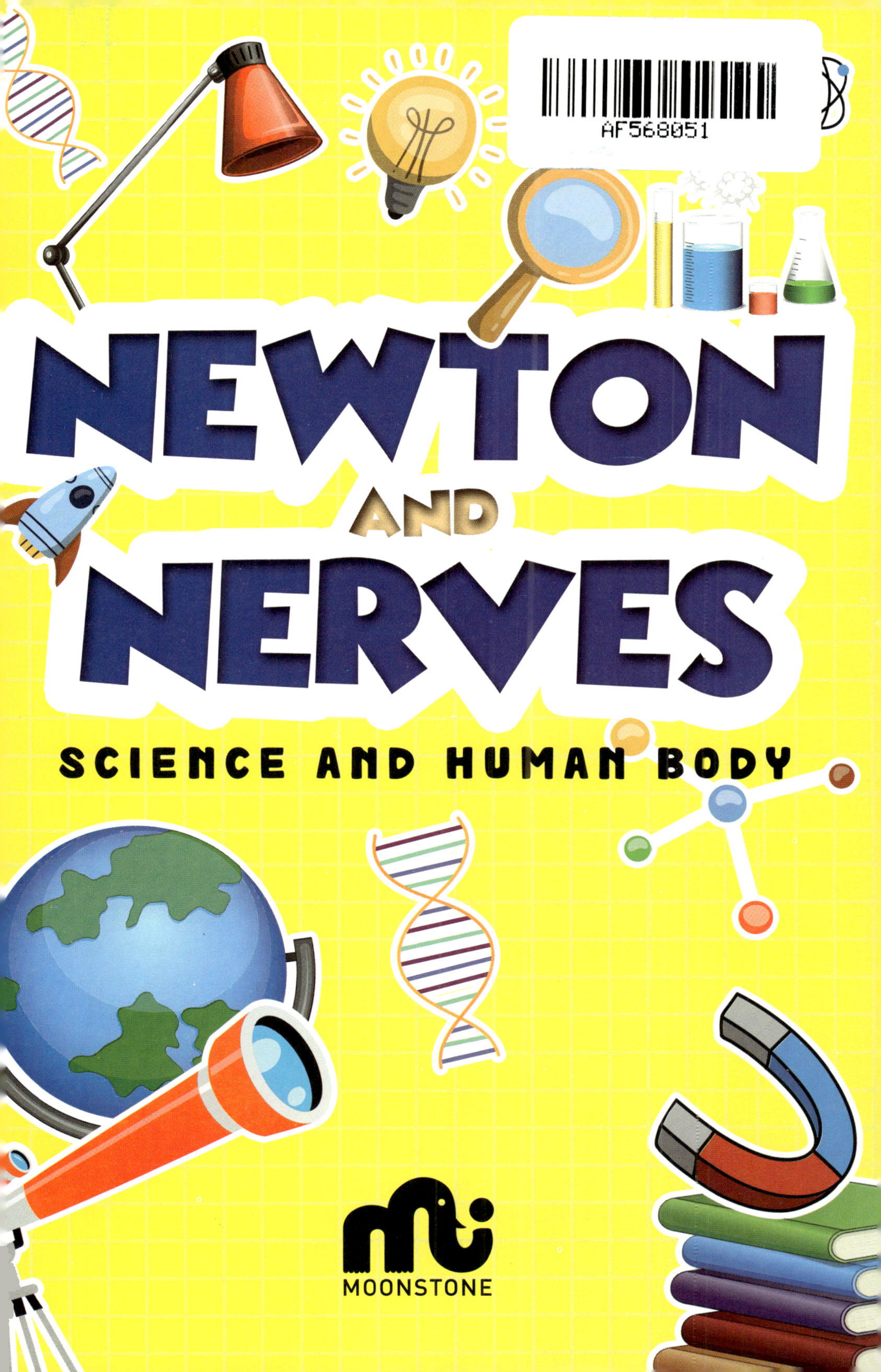

AF568051
NEWTON AND NERVES
SCIENCE AND HUMAN BODY
MOONSTONE

Published in Moonstone
by Rupa Publications India Pvt. Ltd 2024
7/16, Ansari Road, Daryaganj
New Delhi 110002

Sales centres:
Bengaluru Chennai
Hyderabad Jaipur Kathmandu
Kolkata Mumbai Prayagraj

P-ISBN: 978-93-90260-45-4
E-ISBN: 978-93-90260-91-1

First impression 2024

10 9 8 7 6 5 4 3 2 1

Printed in India

CONTENTS

SCIENCE

CONTENTS

HUMAN BODY

SCIENCE AND HUMAN BODY

Introduction

We often wonder why and how things happen. Science answers questions like—how light bulbs glow, how sound travels from one place to another, and why a ball floats in water while a rock sinks.

The word 'science' comes from a Latin word scientia which means knowledge. Science is based on hypotheses, experiments, observations, and results. There are numerous branches of science, including but not limited to physics, chemistry, biology, and astronomy.

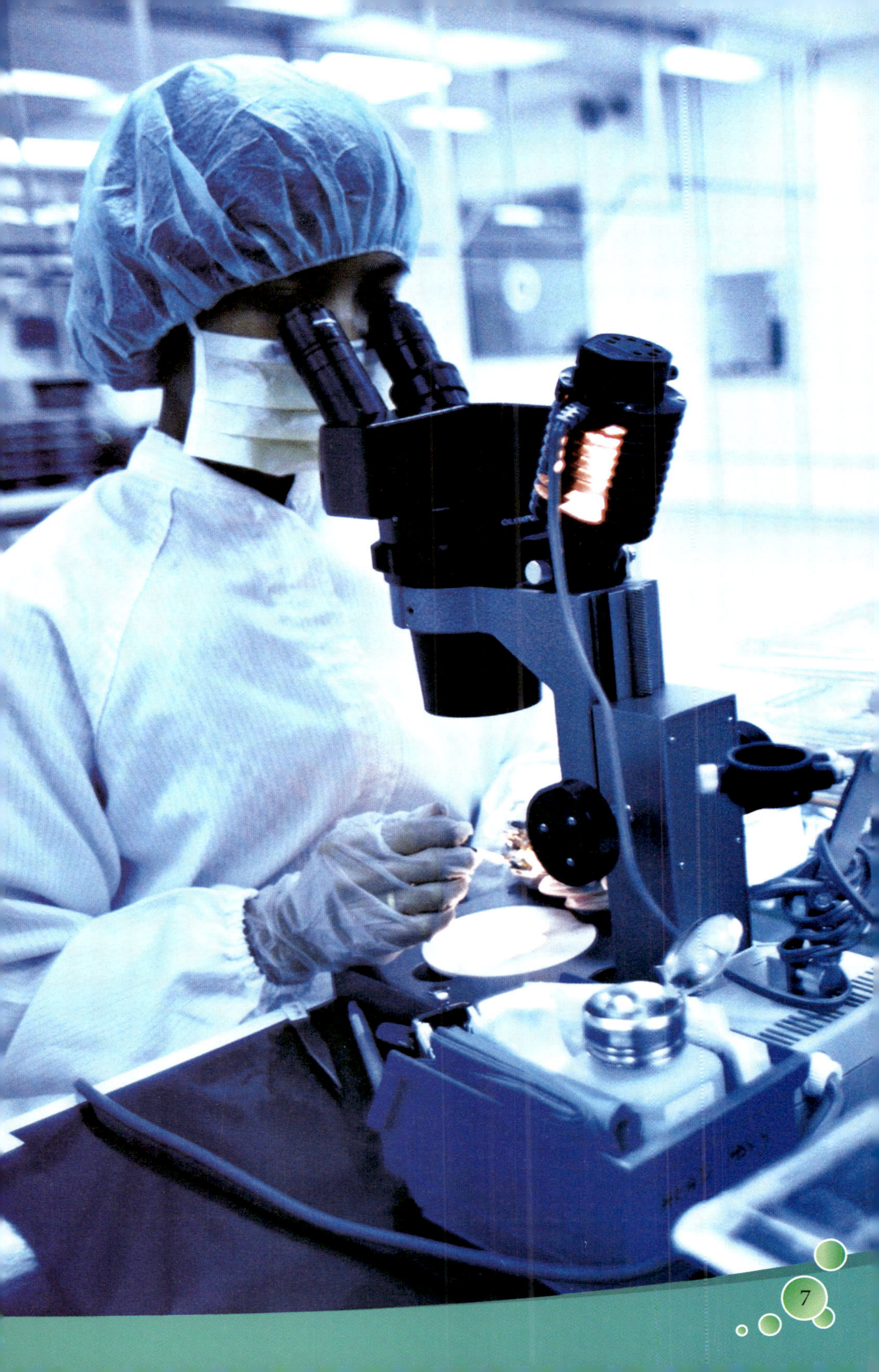

Energy to Work

Energy is the ability to do work. No action is possible without energy. A moving object has kinetic energy. When the object stops, it loses this energy. A standing object has stored energy, which is called potential energy.

Food Gives Us Energy

We can work, speak and move because of the energy we have. The food that we eat, like fruits and vegetables, provides us with energy to work. Our body stores this energy, which we draw on later to keep our bodies working.

Machines Need Energy

Machines also need energy. They get their energy from fuels like petroleum and petrol. Some machines use electricity to operate while others use batteries. Batteries have stored electricity which helps machines to work while the batteries are charged.

Sources of Energy

The Sun is the world's main source of energy. The energy from the Sun comes to the earth in the form of heat and light. As this light and heat energy is used up, it change forms. For example, plants use light energy to make food and grow, and store it as chemical energy.

Forms of Energy

Energy can never be destroyed. It can only change form. Light, sound, heat and electricity are different forms of energy.

Facts

- Half of the total energy used in our homes is used for heating and cooling.
- Bodies need 2,300 daily calories.
- 40% of global energy is from oil.

Stationary object has ________ energy.

Force and Motion

Force is a push or pull. It can start or stop the movement of an object. It also speeds up and slows down moving objects. When we throw a ball, we push the ball to make it move in the air. When we catch a ball, we push our hands against it to slow it down.

When we apply force on a bicycle pedal with our feet, the pedals turn and the wheels move. This force makes the bicycle move.

Twin Force

When a force works in a direction, another force works in its opposite direction. This is called a twin force.

Friction

Friction is a force between two objects or surfaces. It occurs when two surfaces rub together. Friction stops objects from sliding or slipping. Rough surfaces have more friction than smooth surfaces.

Motion

Motion is the movement of an object. An object moves when it is pushed or pulled by a force. Once the object has started moving, force must be applied to make it move faster or slow down.

- Work is the amount of force that is needed to move an object.
- Newton is the unit of force.

What is the movement of an object called?

Light and Shadow

Light makes us see the world. Without light, it is not possible to see anything around us. During the day, most of the world's light comes from the Sun. Electric lights and fire are other sources of light.

White Light

White light is light that comes from the Sun or light bulbs. This white light is actually a mixture of many different colours. When white light is passed through a prism, it scatters into seven different colors. The light waves are bent by the prism.

Reflection

Reflection of light allows us to see objects. It is the bouncing back of light after it falls on an object. Mirrors reflect the light that falls on them, enabling us to see a clear reflection or image.

Shadow

Light from the Sun reaches the Earth's surface in straight lines called rays. When an object blocks these rays, it casts a shadow. The shadow's size depends on the distance between the light and the object and the object's size.

Facts

- Nothing in the world travels faster than light.
- Red, blue, and yellow are its primary colours.
- Sunlight takes eight minutes to reach Earth.

Formation of a rainbow

When sunlight enters tiny raindrops in the air, it splits into a band of seven colours, creating a rainbow. A rainbow can be seen on a sunny day after rain.

? **How many colours are present in white light?**

Hearing Sounds

Sounds are produced by vibrations. When we speak or make sound, these vibrations travel through the air until someone hears them.

Musical Instruments

Musicians produce melodies using instruments. A violin, a stringed instrument, produces sound when a violinist moves a bow across its strings, causing them to vibrate. Similarly, when a drummer hits a drum using hands or sticks, it vibrates, producing sound.

High and Low

Sounds can be high-pitched or low-pitched. The pitch depends upon the frequency of the sound. The number of vibrations produced in a second is the frequency of a sound. Very high-frequency sounds are called ultrasounds. Bats can hear ultrasounds.

- Sound travels at 340 metres/second in air, but faster in water at 1,500 metres/second.
- We hear between 20 to 20,000 vibrations per second.

Echoes

Sounds travel in the form of waves. When these sound waves hit an object or solid surface, they reflect back. The reflected sound we hear is called an echo.

 **What are ultrasounds?**

Heat and Temperature

Heat is a form of energy. When heat energy is added to an object, it becomes hot, and when heat energy is taken away, it becomes cold. Temperature is the measure of how hot or cold an object is.

Measuring Temperature

Temperature can be measured in degrees Celsius (°C) or degrees Fahrenheit (°F). There are various types of thermometres used for this purpose. Electronic thermometres are increasingly common today.

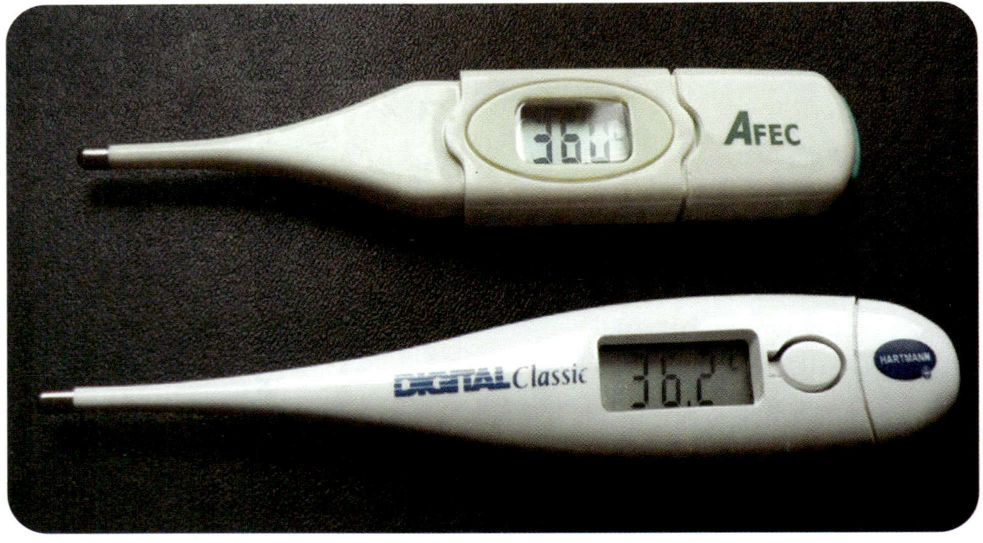

Heat Transfer

In solids, heat is transferred by a process called conduction. Molecules in hot areas pass their energy to those in colder areas, warming them up. Liquids and gases transfer heat through convection. In convection, warm molecules expand and rise, allowing cooler molecules to take their place and warm up. Heat also transfers through radiation. The Sun radiates heat, emitting it as invisible rays into space.

Facts

- Temperatures with a minus sign are below zero.
- A bolometre measures very low temperatures.
- Our body has a normal temperature of 98°F (36.6°C).

Water

Water changes its state from liquid to gas when heated. Water boils when the temperature reaches 100°C and forms water vapour. Water vapour, when cooled, forms tiny droplets of water. When the water is frozen, it transforms into its solid form, called ice.

The transfer of heat in solids is called __________.

Floating and Sinking

Some objects float in water while others sink. When an object is placed in water, it displaces a certain amount of water. If the weight of the object is less than the weight of the displaced water, the object will float. If the object weighs more than the water it displaces, it will sink.

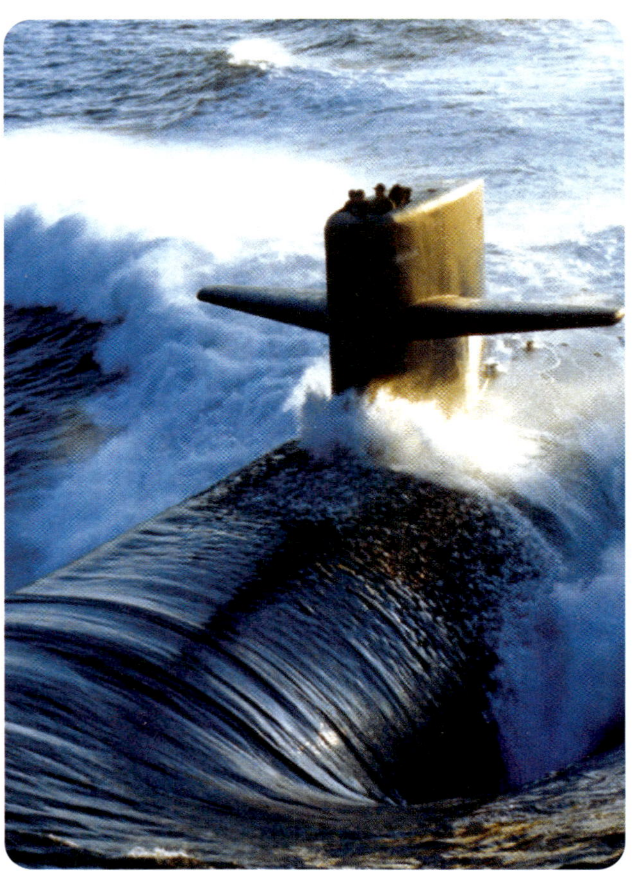

Submarines

Submarines are watercrafts that can operate underwater. They have tanks inside them, which can be filled with water or air. To dive underwater, the tanks are filled with water, making them heavier. To rise to the surface, the water is expelled using compressed air, making them lighter.

Forces Acting on an Object

An object in water experiences two forces—the force of gravity pulling it downward and the buoyant force pushing it upward. The buoyant force is equal to the weight of the water displaced by the object.

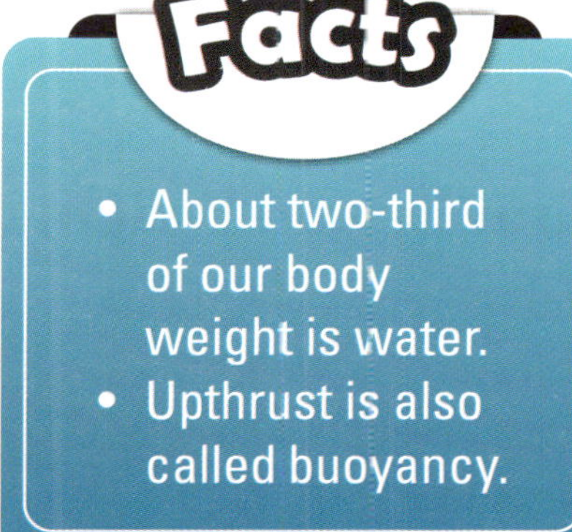

- About two-third of our body weight is water.
- Upthrust is also called buoyancy.

What floats and what sinks?

Dense objects, such as bricks, coins, and solid metal pieces, sink in water. Less dense materials, like pieces of wood, float on water.

? What is a vehicle that can travel underwater called?

Gravity

Gravity is a force that pulls two objects towards each other. Every object in the universe experiences gravity. Earth also exerts gravity. This makes objects fall and keeps us standing on the ground.

Gravity and Weight

Gravity gives weight to objects. The weight of an object measures the amount of gravity acting on it. On the moon's surface, an object weighs less. This is because the moon is smaller than Earth and has weaker gravity.

When we throw a ball in the air, it doesn't remain suspended but falls back to the earth. This happens because gravity pulls it towards the ground.

An astronaut can float in space, high above the earth. Here, they experience weightlessness, as there's very little gravity acting on them. However, some gravity still influences them, causing their motion along the Earth's orbit.

Speed and Weight

When we drop two balls of different weights simultaneously from the same height, both will fall at the same rate and land at the same time. This is because the acceleration due to gravity doesn't depend on the weight of the objects.

Earth's gravity causes rain and snow to fall down on earth. (True or False)

Magnet

Magnets attract certain metals, such as iron, cobalt or nickel. This attraction is because of the magnetic force that magnets have. Materials like wood are not attracted to magnets.

Magnetic Field

A magnet has a magnetic field around it. This field extends as far as the magnet's influence reaches. The magnetic field of a magnet is shown by lines known as magnetic field lines.

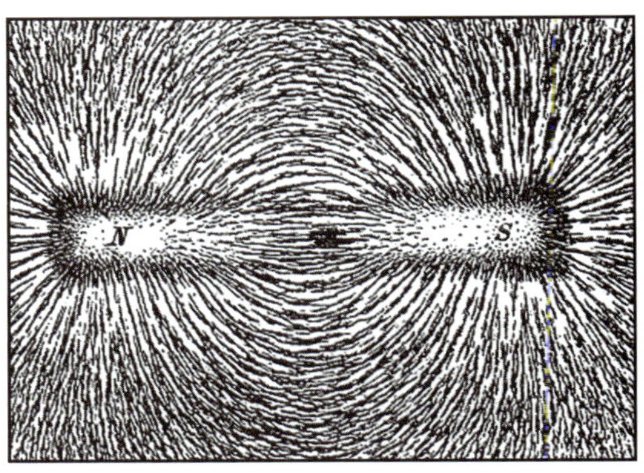

Magnetic Compass

Magnetic compasses are used to determine directions. The earth's magnetic field helps the magnetic compass work. The magnetic needle of the compass swings into the north and south direction according to the earth's north and south pole.

North Pole and South Pole

All magnets have two ends—a north pole and a south pole. When we bring a north pole near a south pole, they attract each other. But when a north pole is brought close to another north pole, they repel each other. This shows that same poles repel each other and opposite poles attract each other.

Maglev

A special train known as Maglev operates on tracks with the help of magnets. Both the train and the track are embedded with magnets. These magnets are positioned in a manner that they repel each other, causing the train to hover above the track.

- The first magnets were known as lodestone.
- Like magnets, the earth also has a north pole and a south pole.

? Name the train that runs on magnetic tracks.

Electricity

Electricity is a form of energy. It makes televisions and radios work. Most of the electricity used in homes is generated in power plants.

Electric Current

Electricity flows along wires and cables. This flow is referred to as electric current. An electric current represents the movement of particles, specifically electrons, carrying tiny packets of electrical energy called charge.

Conductors and Insulators

Most metals allow electricity to flow through them and are known as conductors. Electric wires are generally made from copper, a good conductor. Materials such as wood, plastic and cloth do not allow electricity to flow through them. They are called insulators.

Static Electricity

When materials are rubbed together, static electricity is formed. This is called static because no electric current flows here. Rubbing produces electric charges in the materials and they start attracting other objects. Rub your shoes on a carpet, then place bits of paper near it, and observe the carpet attracting the paper pieces. This is due to static electricity.

- Lightning is a form of static electricity.
- Electric eel is a fish that produces electric shocks for defence and hunting purposes.

Copper is a ________ conductor of electricity.

Atoms and Molecules

All substances are composed of atoms. Atoms are the smallest units of matter. They are so tiny that they can only be viewed with specialised microscopes.

Structure of an Atom

Atoms consist of three types of particles—electrons, protons, and neutrons. The core part is called the nucleus and contains neutrons and protons. Electrons orbit around the nucleus. Every atom contains a significant amount of energy, which is released when its nucleus is split. This energy can be harnessed for electricity generation or to power ships.

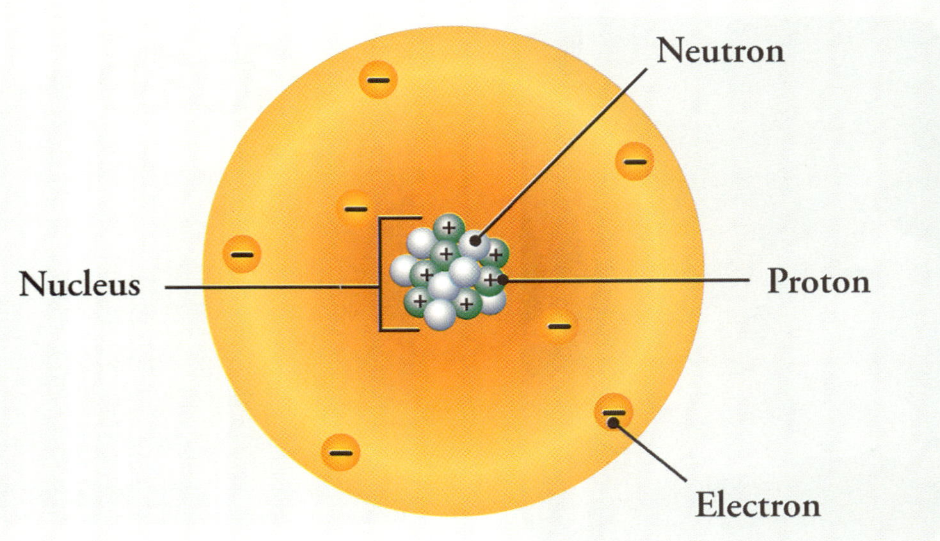

Elements

Substances made up of only one kind of atoms are called elements. More than 90 elements exist in nature. Iron, carbon, oxygen, hydrogen, silver, and gold are some of these elements. Elements cannot be broken down into simpler substances.

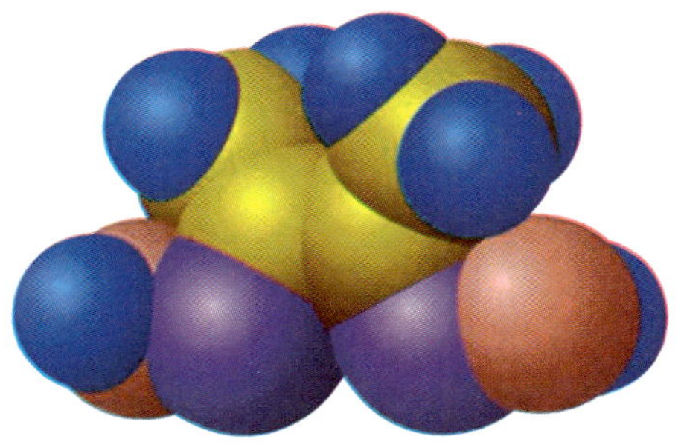

Molecules

Molecules are larger particles. They can be made up of the same or different kinds of atoms. For example, each molecule of water has two atoms of hydrogen and one atom of oxygen.

Compounds

Water is a chemical compound. It is formed from the same kind of molecules with each molecule having hydrogen and oxygen. These molecules are held together by bonds between the atoms.

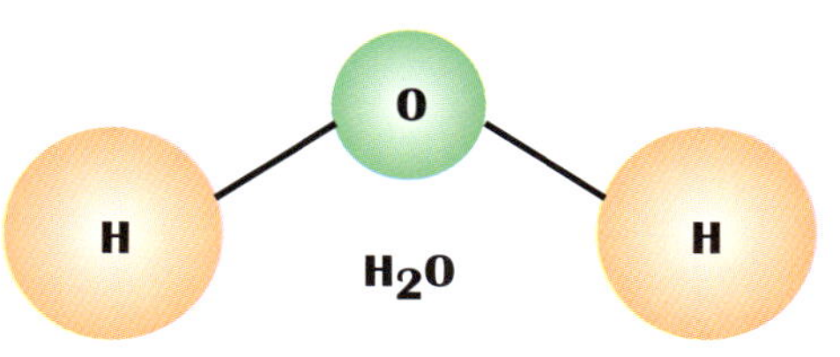

- John Dalton defined atoms as the tiniest particles.
- Protons are positively charged; electrons are negative. Opposite charges bond atoms.

An atom is made up of electrons, ______ and neutrons.

Solid, Liquid, and Gas

Matter exists in three states — solid, liquid, and gas. Solids have a fixed shape, but liquids and gases take the shape of their container and can flow from place to place.

Moving Molecules

Matter consists of tiny particles called molecules. In solids, molecules are tightly packed, restricting movement and shape change. In liquids, molecules have more space, allowing movement. In gases, molecules move freely without confinement.

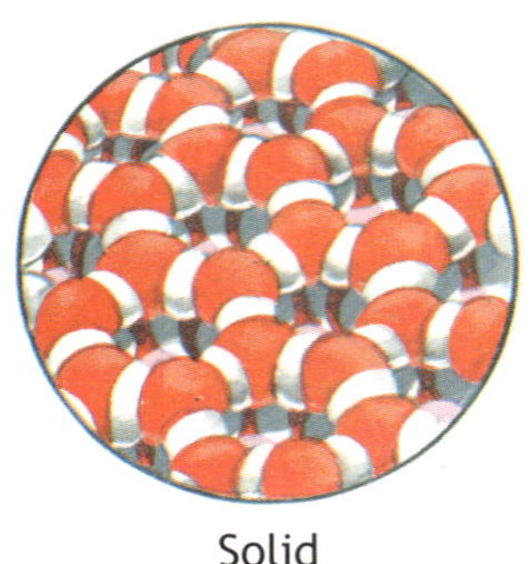
Solid

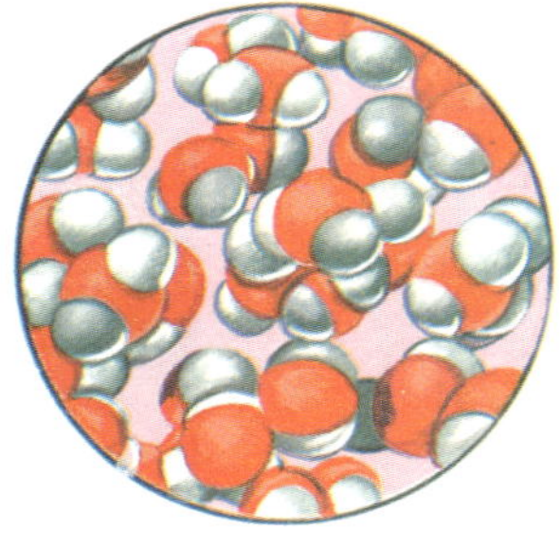
Liquid

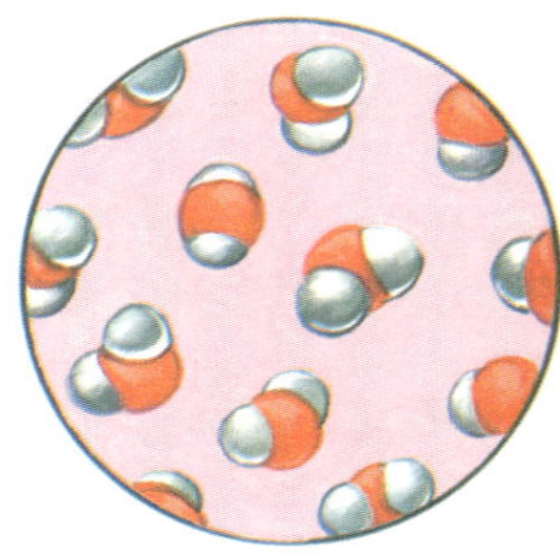
Gas

Diamond and Graphite

Diamonds and graphite are both carbon forms but have different molecular arrangements. Diamonds, renowned as the world's hardest materials, are commonly used in jewellery and for cutting purposes. On the other hand, graphite is significantly softer.

Solid

Altering the shape of solids is a challenging task. Typically, solids retain their form, resisting changes even when subjected to bending, twisting, or stretching. However, when exposed to high temperatures, a solid might transform. Notably, iron, as a solid example, begins to melt when temperatures exceed 1500°C.

- A diamond can only be cut by another diamond.
- Thick liquids like honey, flow slower than thin liquids because they have higher viscosity.

What is the hardest substance in the world?

Metals and Non-Metals

The most commonly used objects, like paper clips, jewellery, and electronics, are made of metals such as iron, gold, and aluminium. All life forms on Earth contain carbon, a non-metal. Other non-metals, like hydrogen and oxygen, combine to form water.

Strong Metals

Metals are solid, robust substances. They aren't easily broken. Metals are excellent conductors of electricity and heat.

Non-Metals

Non-metals can exist as solids, liquids, or gases. Oxygen and nitrogen are gaseous non-metals. They don't conduct electricity. Abundant amounts of non-metals, like carbon and oxygen, are found in all living things.

- Mercury is the only metal that is liquid at room temperature.
- Metalloids are elements with properties of both metals and non-metals.

Steel

Steel is a mixture of a metal (iron) and non-metal (carbon). It is made by melting iron and carbon together to make a stronger end product. Steel is known as an alloy.

Metal Extraction

Some rocks contain substances called as ores. Ores are a combination of metals and oxygen. When ores are heated in a furnace, a reaction occurs removing the oxygen. This process produces a pure metal, which is then used to make objects.

Is gold a non-metal?

Mixtures and Solutions

Mixtures and solutions are everywhere around us. Anything made up of two or more things is a mixture. Solutions are also special type of mixtures.

What is a Mixture?

Mixtures are made up of several substances. These substances do not make a new substance and can be physically separated.

Types of Mixtures

There are two types of mixtures-heterogeneous and homogeneous. Heterogeneous mixtures are not uniform in composition. Salad is a good example of heterogeneous mixture. On the other hand, homogeneous mixtures are uniform in composition. Air is an example of homogeneous mixture.

What is a Solution?

Solutions are homogeneous mixtures. But unlike mixtures, substances in solution are not easily separable. A solution is made up of a solvent and a solute. A solute is something that dissolves in a solvent. For example, sugar dissolves in water; here, sugar is the solute and water is the solvent.

Types of Solution

Solutions can be divided into two types – saturated solution and unsaturated solution. Saturated solution is a solution in which a solvent cannot dissolve any more solute. Unsaturated solutions are those solutions in which a solvent can still dissolve more solute.

- An alloy is a type of homogeneous mixture.
- Filtering is a common method to separate heterogeneous mixtures.
- Water, a universal solvent, dissolves many substances.

? An alloy is a ______ mixture.

Materials Around Us

We use many things in our daily lives. These things are made from different materials such as plastic, wood, metal and cloth. Tools are made from metals because metals are strong and can be transformed into different shapes.

Plastic

Bottles, buckets, cups, balls, bags and many other things are made from plastic. Plastic can be easily moulded into any shape by heating.

Pottery

Pottery items like cups, plates and pots are made from clay. Clay is soft earth matter. It is given a shape and baked at high temperatures to make pottery.

Glass

Glass is made from a mineral found in sand called quartz. Other chemical compounds, such as soda (sodium carbonate) and lime (calcium oxide), are mixed with sand and heated until the mixture melts into a liquid. As the liquid cools, it hardens and turns into glass.

Recycling is Good

We should recycle used materials. This will save the earth's natural resources and energy. Paper, glass, metal and plastic are all recyclable materials.

Facts

- Bronze is an alloy made by mixing copper and tin.
- Coloured glasses are made by adding copper, nickel or cobalt compounds.

What is glass made from?

Simple Machines

Machines are tools that help us do work. They use force to make tasks easy. Machines that have few or no moving parts are easy to use. These machines are called simple machines.

Types of Simple Machines

We use simple machines in our day-to-day activities. A few of the commonly used simple machines are:

- Screws, pulleys, and gears are simple machines.
- Pulleys lift loads; gears adjust speed and direction; screws hold or press materials together.

Lever

A lever consists of a bar that rests on a fulcrum that does not move. It is used for lifting heavy loads. Seesaw is an example of a lever.

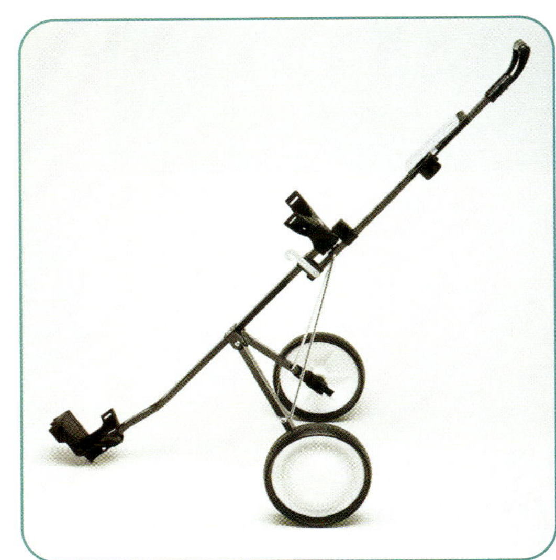

Inclined Plane

An inclined plane is a simple machine with a slanted surface. The slanting surface connects the lower level to the higher level to make moving objects easier. Ramps and stairs are inclined planes.

Wedge

A wedge is made up of two inclined planes. It is used either to split an object or raise an object. For example, door wedge and axe are wedges.

Pulley

A pulley is made up of a wheel and a rope. The rope is fitted into the grooved rim of the wheel. One part of the rope is attached to the load, while the other is used for pulling it. A flagpole uses a pulley system.

Wheel and Axle

Wheel and axle work together as simple machines. A wheel turns around at its centre on a bar called axle. They are used to carry heavy weights and move things faster. All transport vehicles have wheels that move around an axle.

An axe is an example of ________. (lever/wedge)

Science in Action

Technology represents the practical application of scientific knowledge. It is evident in homes, schools, offices, banks, and hospitals. Common technological tools include computers, cameras, radios, televisions, and cars, while bridges, dams, weapons, aeroplanes, and satellites are advanced applications.

Simple Technology

Historically, early humans utilised basic technology. They crafted tools for hunting from small stone pieces and built homes using natural materials like wood, clay, and straw.

Modern Technology

Contemporary structures such as dams, bridges, buildings, and houses are created using advanced technological techniques. Engineers, responsible for their design and construction, ensure the use of high-quality materials and maintain the safety and structural integrity of these buildings.

Facts

- Intelsat is one of the world's largest communication satellite network.
- Intelsat passes on communications around the world with the help of ground stations in more than 100 countries.

Satellite Technology

Artificial satellites are man-made objects that orbit planets and travel through space. There are various types, among which communication satellites are a notable category. They facilitate global communication by transmitting signals for telephone, television, and radio services. Ground-based earth stations send signals to these satellites, which are then relayed back to other earth stations. This technology significantly contributes to connecting the world more closely.

Artificial satellites orbit around planets. (True or False)

Studying Science

Scientists study various fields of science, employing the scientific method to explore, discover, and innovate. New inventions often result from the experiments conducted by scientists.

Branches of Science

The major branches of science include physics, chemistry, and biology. Physicists examine particles, states of matter, electricity, and phenomena like heat, light, and sound. Biologists focus on living organisms, studying microorganisms in labs to develop disease treatments. Chemists investigate elements, compounds, and chemicals, and they synthesise new chemical substances.

Facts

- Medical scientists develop new medicines and medical equipment for doctors.
- Laboratories are specialised facilities for scientific experiments.
- Oceanography studies oceans and seas.

Branches of Science	Scientists	What do they study
Chemistry	Chemist	The study of chemical components and properties of matter.
Physics	Physicist	The study of matter and its properties.
Astronomy	Astronomer	The study of the sun, planets, and other objects in the universe.
Ecology	Ecologist	The study of living beings and their interaction with the environment.
Environmental science	Environmentalist	The study of physical, chemical and biological components of the environment.
Biology	Biologist	The study of living beings and their behaviour.
Botany	Botanist	The study of plants.
Zoology	Zoologist	The study of animals.
Medicine	Doctor	The branch of science that deals with the health of living beings and treatment of diseases.
Geology	Geologist	The study of the Earth, including its materials, processes, and history.

What is a person who studies physics called?

Famous Scientists

Scientists are people who specialise in the fields of science – astronomy, chemistry, physics, etc. Some of the greatest scientists like Newton, Einstein and Edison changed the world with their inventions and discoveries.

Isaac Newton

Isaac Newton was an English mathematician, astronomer and physicist. He formulated the Law of Universal Gravitation, which states that that all objects in the universe attract each other with a force directly proportional to their mass product and inversely proportional to the square of their distance. Newton is also famously known for his contribution in optics. He showed that white light is made up of seven colours with the help of prism. He invented a working reflective telescope.

Facts

- Newton held the Lucasian Chair of Mathematics at Cambridge.
- Thomas Edison became partially deaf at the age of twelve because of an illness.
- Pasteur established germ theory in disease causation.

Thomas Edison

Thomas Edison was an American inventor. He invented and developed many devices that changed everyday life. Edison invented the phonograph in 1877 and the incandescent light bulb in 1879. During his life, Edison invented 1093 items and received patents for all of them.

Albert Einstein

Albert Einstein was one of the greatest scientists of all time. He developed the theory of relativity which states that mass and energy to an extent are interchangeable and that mass and time can vary. He explained it by the equation, $E = mc2$, where E is energy, m is mass and c is the speed of light. He was awarded the Nobel Prize for physics in 1921.

? Who discovered gravity?

Glossary

Petrol: a liquid fuel used in automobiles

Pedal: a simple machine used in a bicycle; a lever activated by a foot

Prism: it's a solid geometric figure whose two end faces are similar, equal, and parallel rectilinear figures, and whose sides are parallelograms

Invisible: something that cannot be seen

Compress: to force into less space; to press together

Astronaut: a person who is trained to travel into outer space

Track: a pair of parallel metal rails where trains run

Power plant: a building where electricity is generated

Furnace: a closed container where heat is produced by burning fuel

Microscope: an instrument used for observing very tiny objects

Natural resources: water, land, coal and oil that are supplied by nature

Transmission: transferring or sending

Microorganism: tiny organism that can only be seen through a microscope, such as bacteria

Watercraft: a vehicle that can run on water

Patent: a legal right to exclude others from making, using, or selling an invention for a limited period, not just a right to manufacture and sell.

Recycle: to treat or process in order to use again

Alloy: a mixture of metals, or metals with non-metals

Compass: an equipment with a needle that always points magnetic north, used in finding way

Calorie: a unit measuring energy we get from food

Aluminum: a light silver colored metal

Incandescent: to give out light because of heat

Nucleus: the central part of an atom

Satellite: an object that is sent into space to orbit the earth to receive and send information

Answers

Page No. 9	Potential
Page No. 11	Motion
Page No. 13	Seven
Page No. 15	High frequency sounds
Page No. 17	Conduction
Page No. 19	Submarine
Page No. 21	True
Page No. 23	Maglev train
Page No. 25	Good
Page No. 27	Protons
Page No. 29	Diamond
Page No. 31	No
Page No. 33	Homogeneous
Page No. 35	Quartz
Page No. 37	Wedge
Page No. 39	True
Page No. 41	Physicist
Page No. 43	Isaac Newton

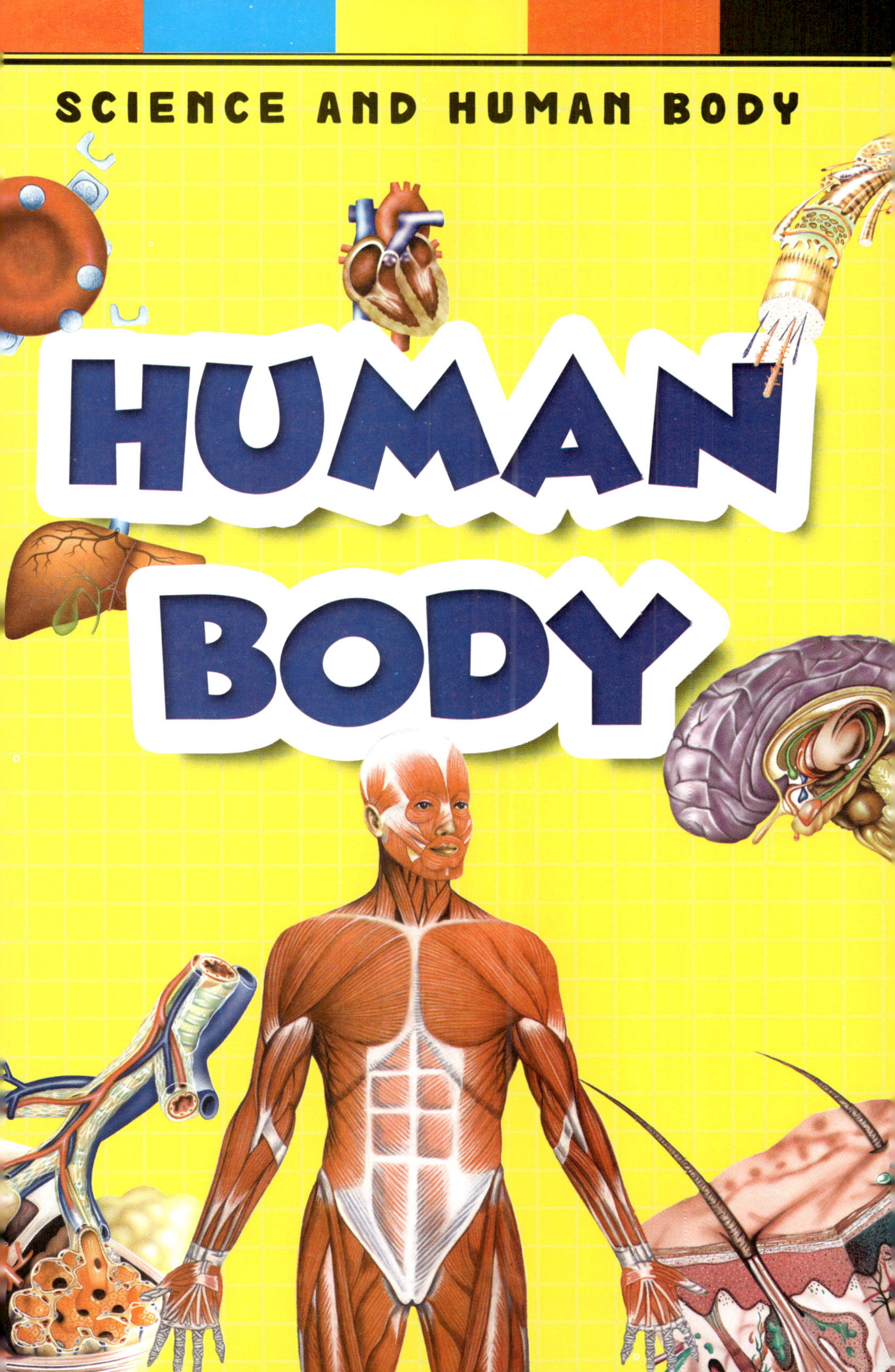
SCIENCE AND HUMAN BODY
HUMAN
BODY

Introduction

Human beings possess a complex body structure composed of an intricate network of multiple organ systems. These systems function in coordination, maintaining harmony with each other to ensure the proper functioning of the body.

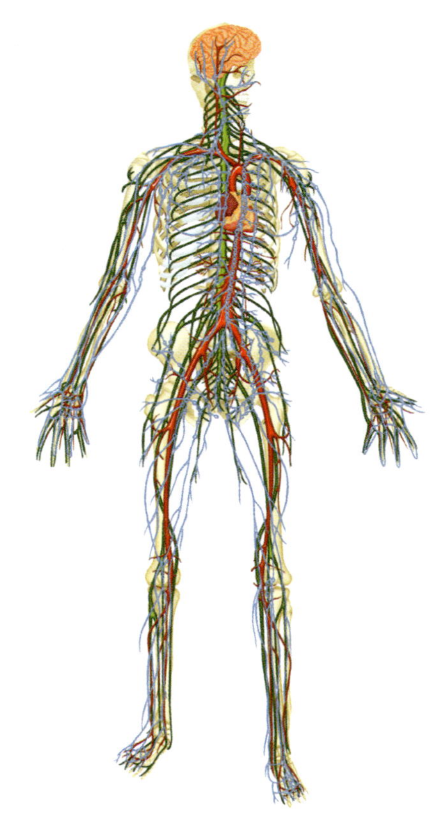

The human body is built upon a bony framework, which, in conjunction with muscles, facilitates movement. Additionally, the bones protect various internal organs, which control different body systems.

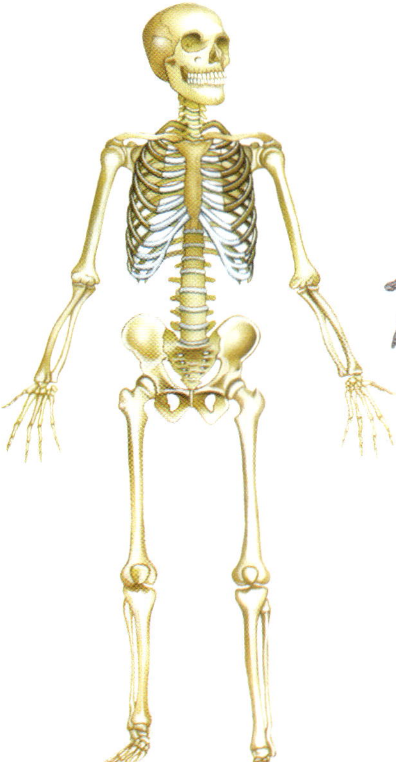

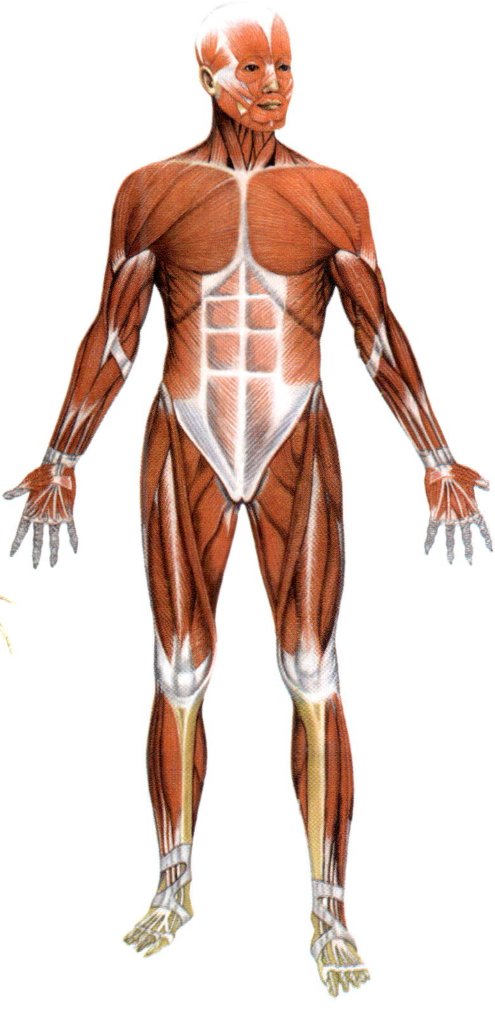

Building Blocks

Cells constitute the building blocks of the human body. Visible only under a microscope, they form the basis of all living organisms, from unicellular life forms to complex multicellular. It is estimated that an adult human body contains approximately 30 to 100 trillion cells.

Cell Structure

All cells are surrounded by a semi-permeable membrane known as the plasma membrane. The interior of a cell is divided into the nucleus and the cytoplasm. The nucleus lies at the centre of the cell. It is the control centre of the cell. It contains all the information necessary for the cell to function. The cytoplasm is a semi-transparent fluid that fills the cell. Smaller organelles float in the cytoplasm.

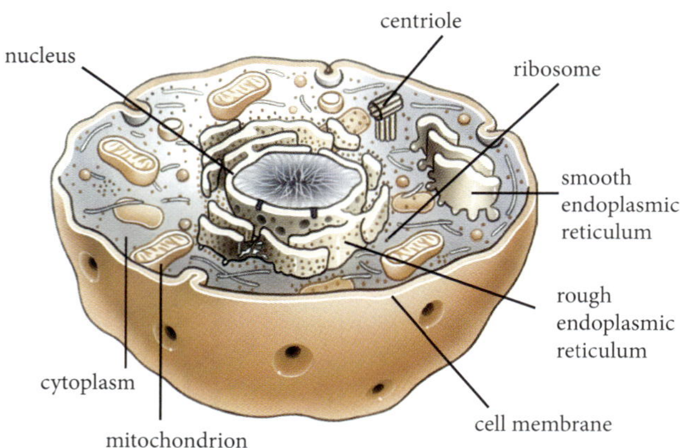

Cell Division

Cells divide to produce new cells. First, the cell makes a copy of its genetic information inside the nucleus. Then the nucleus divides into two parts. Finally the cytoplasm divides to produce two identical daughter cells. The daughter cells divide further for growth and repair.

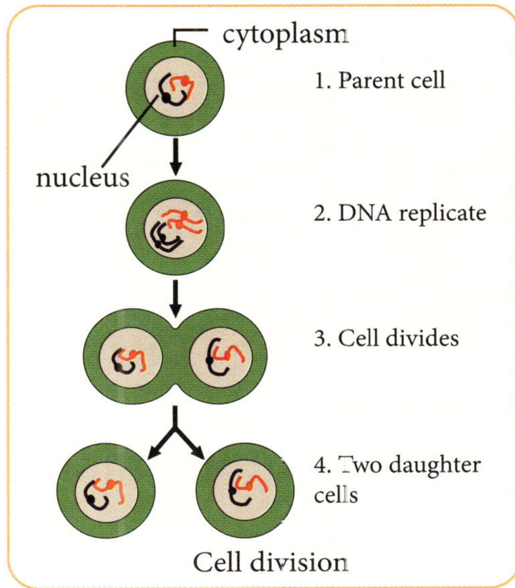

Cell division

Types of Cell

Each part of the body is made up of a special type of cells, depending on their functions. For example, the nervous system is made up of nerve cells. Each cell type has its own shape and size. For instance, nerve cells are long in shape, and blood cells are round.

- An adult human body is made up of 100 trillion cells.
- A cell's organelles are also known as "little organs."
- On an average, a cell measures 0.005 millimetres (0.0002 inches) in diametre.

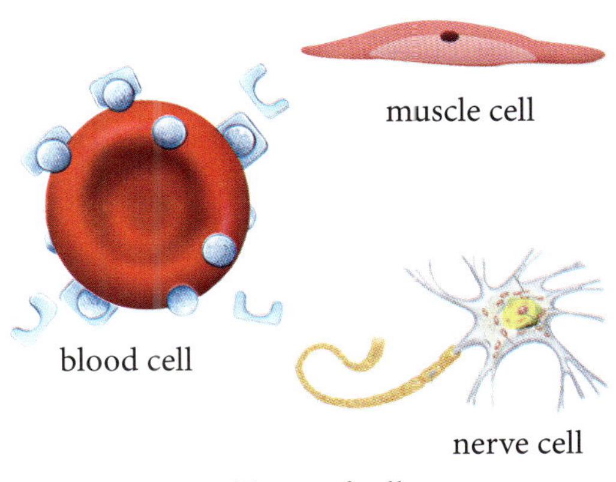

Types of cells

 **Nucleus lies at the _______ of the cell.**

Tissues and Organs

Tissues are groups of cells joined together. The cells in a tissue have the same structure and function. Different types of tissue join together to form different organs. Organs, in turn, group together to form organ systems.

Organs

Two or more types of tissue join to make an organ. The heart, kidneys, liver, lungs, stomach, and skin are the major organs in our body. Each organ performs its own function and also works together with other organs to make the body run smoothly.

Types of Tissue

There are different types of tissue. Connective tissues bind and support all parts of the body. Muscle tissues help in the movement of the body and protect the bones and joints. Nerve tissues send and receive messages from one part of the body to another.

Nerve tissue

Connective tissue

Muscle tissue

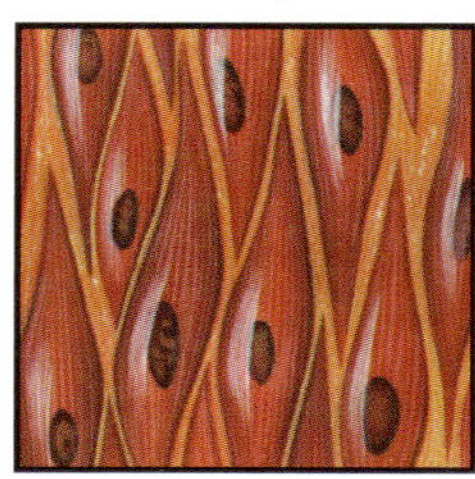

Organ Systems

When a group of organs function together, they form an organ system. The heart and blood vessels work together in the circulatory system. The digestive system includes the stomach, liver and intestines. The muscular system is made of muscles while the skeletal system is made of bones.

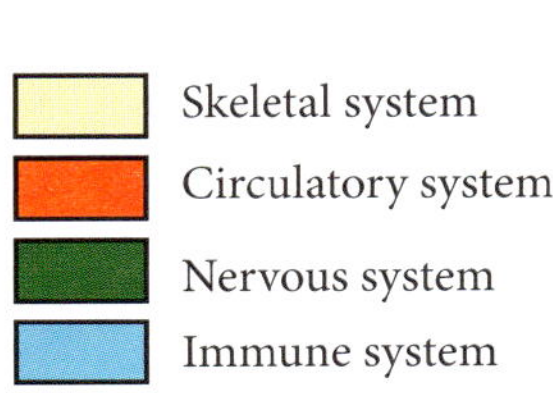

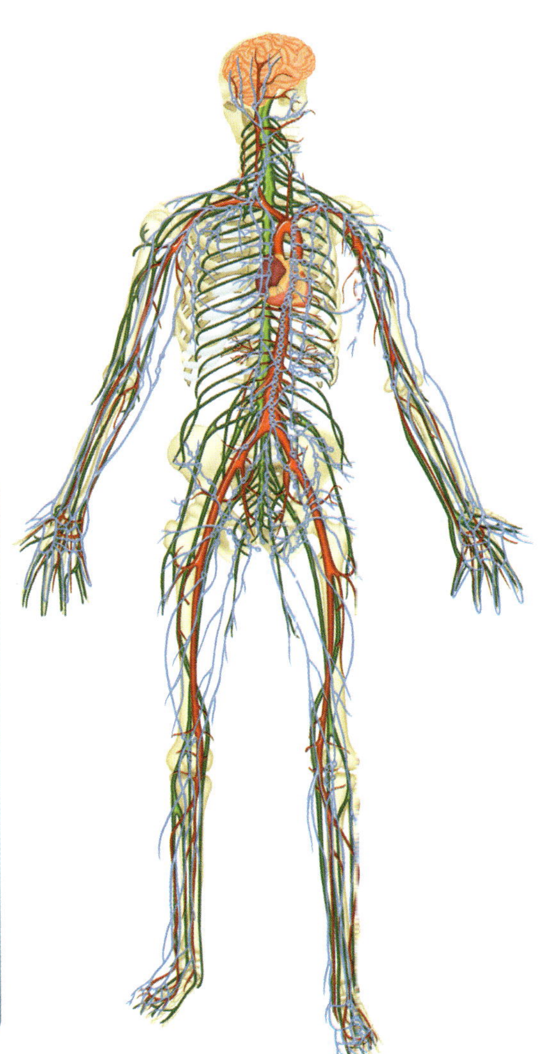

Major systems of the body

- Recent research reveals the appendix may have roles in gut immunity, contradicting past beliefs of its insignificance.
- The skin is the largest organ of the human body.

What is the largest organ in the human body?

See, Smell and Hear

Eyes, nose and ears are the three major sense organs. They gather information from our surroundings and send it to the brain. The brain then processes this information and allows us to see, smell and hear.

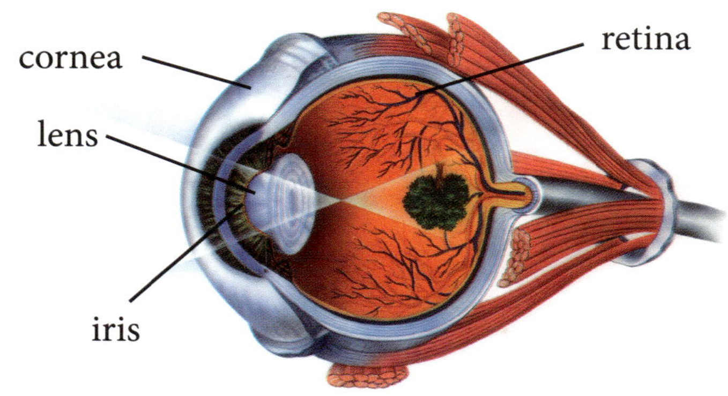

Cross-section of eye

The Sense of Sight

The cornea is the outermost part of the eye. Light enters the eye through the cornea and then passes through the pupil and iris to reach the lens. The lens focuses the light onto the retina—the innermost layer of the eye. The retina contains millions of light-sensitive cells known as rods and cones, which send signals to the brain. The brain converts these signals into images for us to see.

The Sense of Smell

There are many odour particles in the air. Foods, perfumes, and smoke are examples of things that can produce these particles. They enter the nose through the nostrils and reach the nasal cavity, where special cells send smell signals to the brain. The brain then helps us identify the smell.

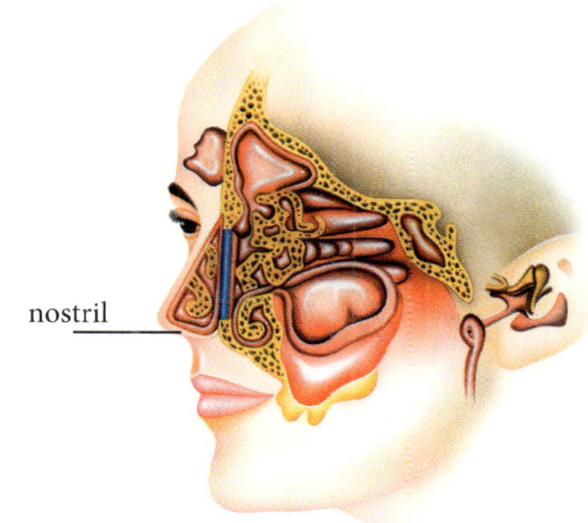

Nose

- Tears wash away germs and dust from the eyes.
- Most people blink their eyes every 2 to 10 seconds.
- Animals can hear more sounds than human beings can.
- Sense of smell is also called olfaction.

The Sense of Hearing

The ear has three parts—the outer, middle, and inner ear. The outer ear catches sound waves present in the air. These waves are converted into vibrations by the eardrum. These vibrations create sound signals, which are sent to the brain by tiny hair present in the inner ear. The brain then helps us identify the sounds.

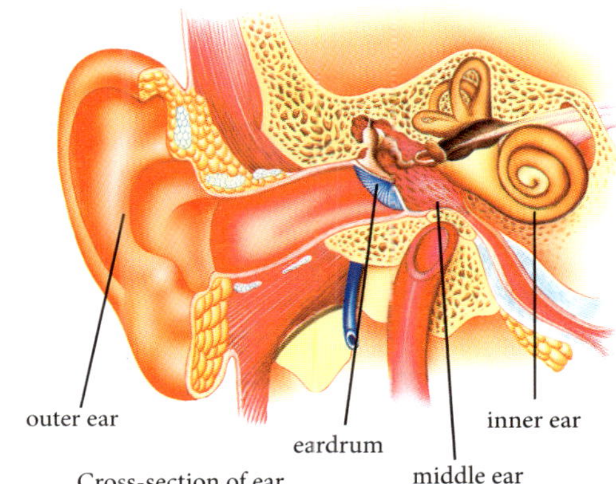

Cross-section of ear

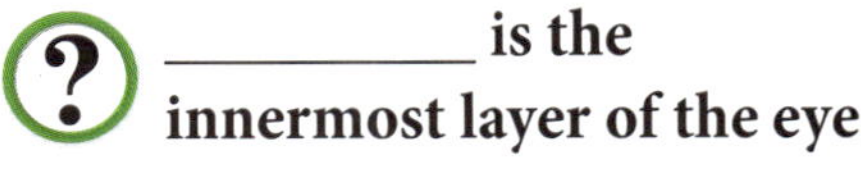

__________ is the innermost layer of the eye.

Taste and Touch

Tongue and skin are the sense organs of taste and touch. The taste buds found on the tongue detect the taste of what we eat and drink. The tongue also helps in talking, chewing, swallowing and singing. Skin covers and protects the organs, bones and muscles of our bodies.

The Sense of Taste

There are thousands of taste buds on the tongue. Sweet, bitter, sour, and salty are the major groups of taste buds. Each taste bud has cells with tiny, sensitive nerve fibres. When we eat something, these fibres send messages to the brain. The brain then identifies the taste.

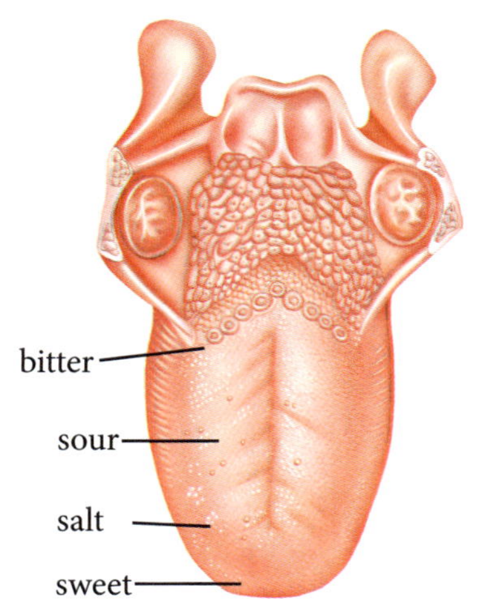

Structure of Tongue

- The average life of a taste bud is 10 days.
- An adult has more than 1.86 square metres (almost 21 square feet) of skin.
- We shed 30,000 to 40,000 dead cells every minute from our body.

The Sense of Touch

Our skin has sensitive nerve endings below its surface. They react immediately to heat, cold, pain, and pressure and quickly send messages to the brain. The brain then helps us identify the texture and temperature of the object.

Skin Layers

The skin is made up of three layers—epidermis (the outermost layer), dermis (the next layer) and a fat layer (the innermost layer). The epidermis contains dead and tough cells that cover and protect the body. The dermis contains the blood vessels, nerve endings, and glands. The fat layer helps the body stay warm.

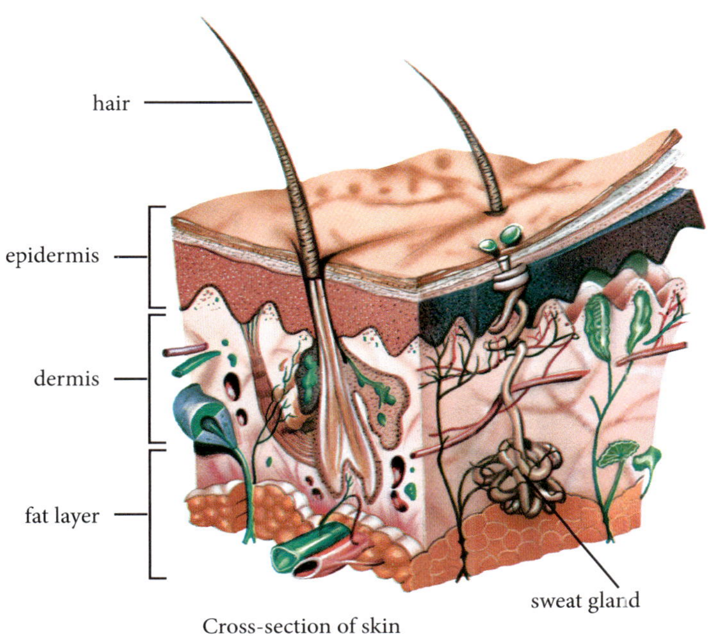

Cross-section of skin

What is the outermost layer of skin called?

Teeth, Hair and Nails

Teeth are small bone-like structures that grow on the jaws inside the mouth. We use our teeth to chew and crush food. Hairs are thread-like structures that cover most parts of the body while nails are horn-like structures on the tips of the fingers and toes.

Structure of Teeth

The root and crown are the major parts of a tooth. The root is where a tooth is fixed to the tooth socket, and the crown is what is visible. The crown is covered with enamel. It protects the inside of the tooth.

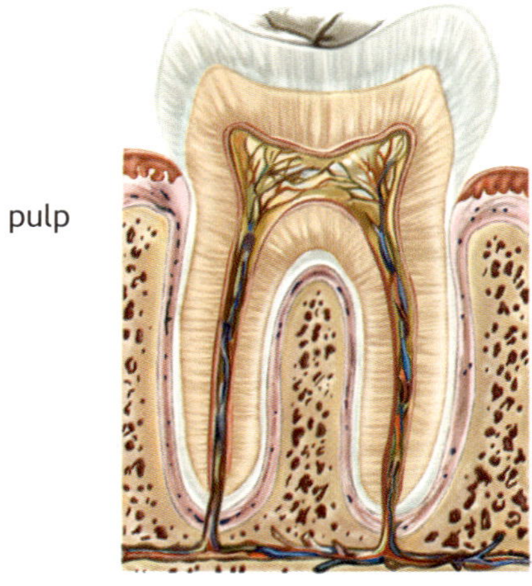

Structure of a Tooth

- Enamel is the hardest substance in the human body.
- Hair on the head grows about 1.27 centimetres (0.5 inches) every month.
- Teeth are first visible when a baby is about 6 to 12 months old.

Nails

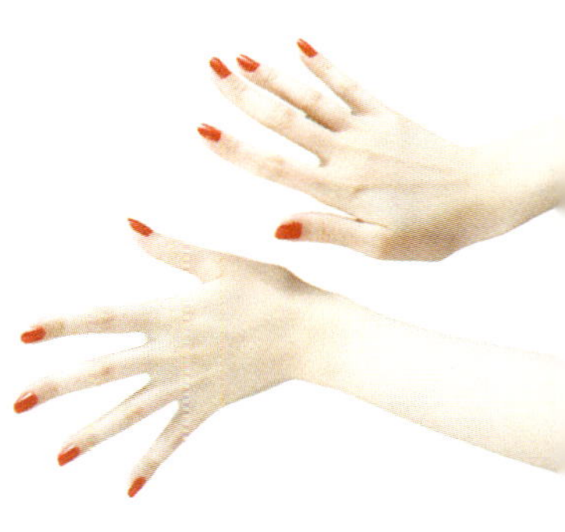

Nails are made of keratin. They grow from the nail root that lies below the cuticle. The new nail cells push out the old nail cells. Nails grow about 2.5 millimetres (0.1 inch) in a month.

Hair All Over

Hair covers almost all parts of the body except the lips, the palms of the hands, and the soles of the feet. Hair grows from the hair root beneath the surface of the skin. The hair root is found inside a small tube called a hair follicle. Here the cells group together to form keratin—a hard protein from which hair is made.

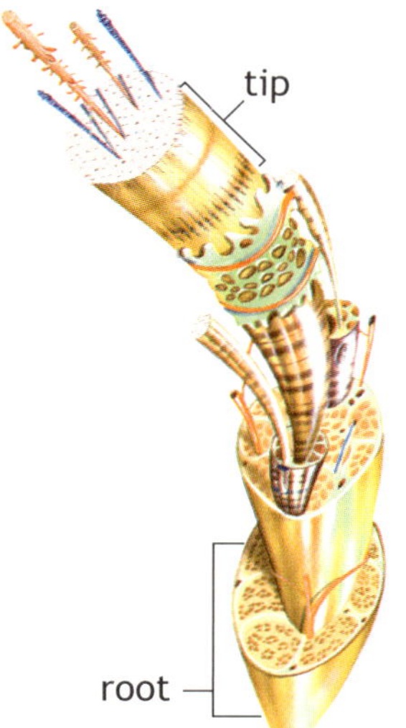

Structure of Hair

? Nails are made of keratin. (True or False)

Digesting Food

The food we eat provides energy and helps us grow. It breaks down into simpler substances. The body then uses it to gain energy. The process of breaking down food to gain energy is called digestion.

Taking in Food

We take in food from the mouth. Teeth crush and cut the food, and the tongue mixes it with saliva. The food then goes down to the stomach through the food pipe, or oesophagus. Here, the food is broken down into a liquid mixture, or paste. The paste is mixed even more with the help of stomach juices.

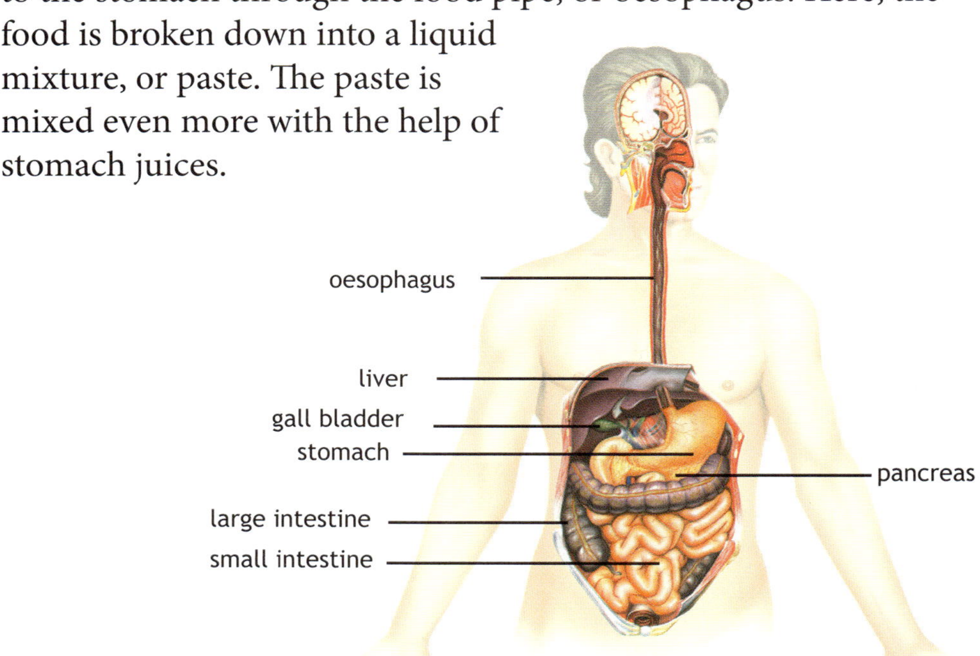

Digestive system

Small Intestine

The liquid mixture made in the stomach slowly reaches the small intestine. Here the absorption of nutrients, such as proteins, vitamins, and fats takes place. These nutrients get mixed with blood, which carries them to different parts of the body.

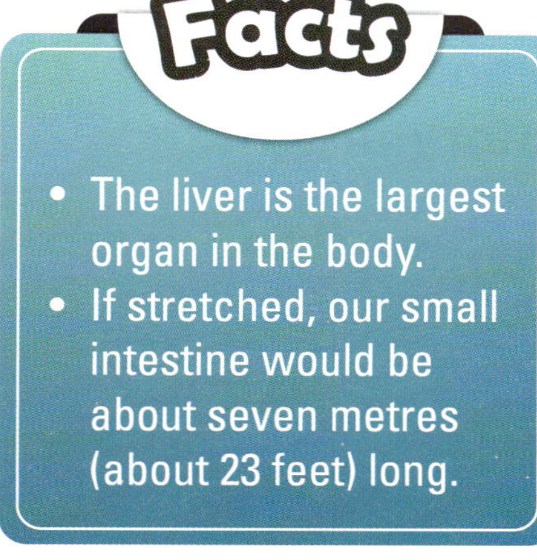

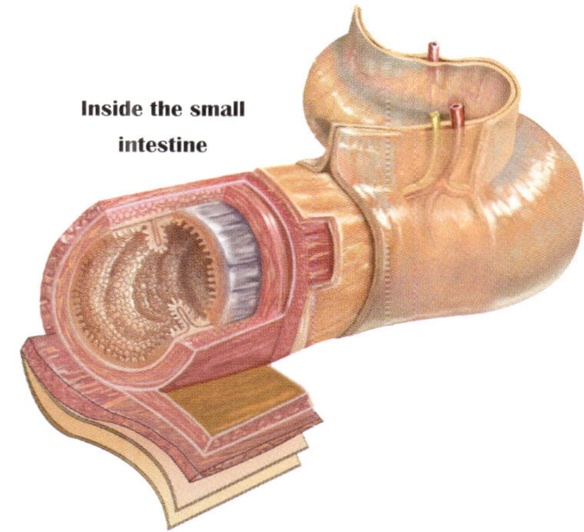

Helping Organs

The pancreas, liver, and gall bladder are the auxiliary organs of the digestive system. They release and send acidic juices to the small intestine to help in the digestion of food and the absorption of nutrients. Pancreatic juices digest the fat protein, and the juices secreted by the liver help the body to absorb fat.

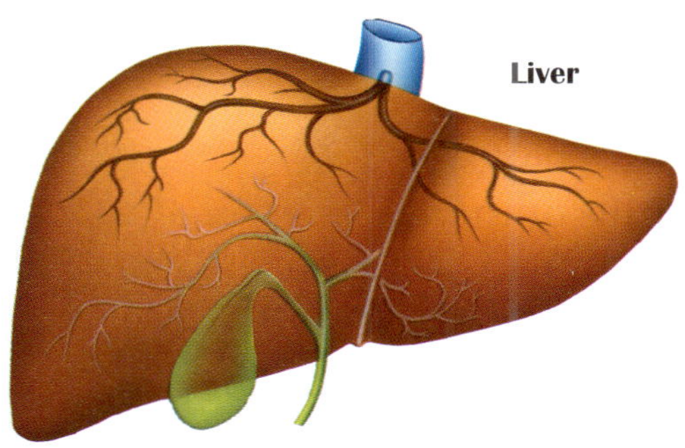

What is the common name of oesophagus?

Breathing Air

We inhale oxygen from the air. The respiratory system helps us to inhale oxygen and release carbon dioxide from our body. The nose and lungs are the main respiratory organs.

Respiratory System

We breathe air through the nose and mouth. The air is then taken to the lungs through the trachea (windpipe). The trachea branches off into the left and the right lungs. The two branches, called the bronchi, enter the lungs and spread into thousands of smaller tubes called bronchioles. The bronchioles carry oxygen into the lungs. Each bronchiole ends in tiny air sacs called alveoli. Oxygen enters blood through the thin walls of the alveoli while carbon dioxide also enters the lungs through the same path.

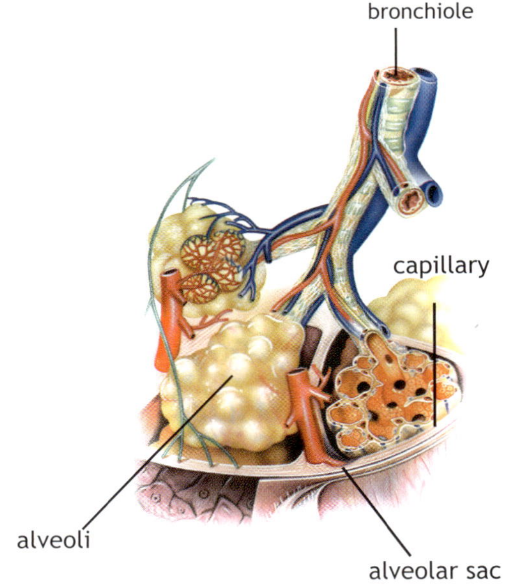

Facts

- The left lung is slightly smaller than the right lung to make space for the heart.
- There are about 30,000 bronchioles in each lung.

Air In and Out

The diaphragm is a sheet of muscles below the lungs that separates the chest from the abdomen. It helps in breathing air in and out with the help of other muscles.

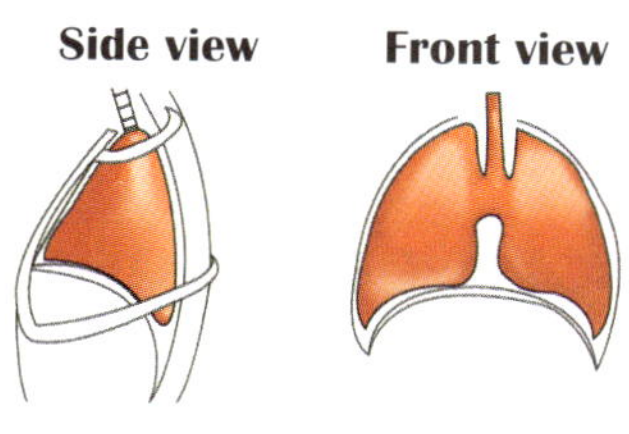

Breathing in flattens the diaphragm, creating space for the lungs to expand and take air in.

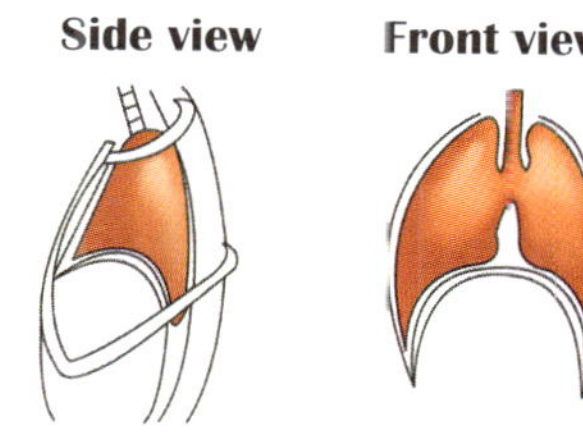

Breathing out relaxes the diaphragm and allows the lungs to contract, pushing air out.

Gas Exchange

Many tiny blood vessels, or capillaries, surround the small air sacs known as alveoli. It is here that the exchange of gases between the lungs and the blood occurs: oxygen is inhaled into the alveoli and then diffuses into the blood, while carbon dioxide is passed from the blood to the alveoli to be exhaled.

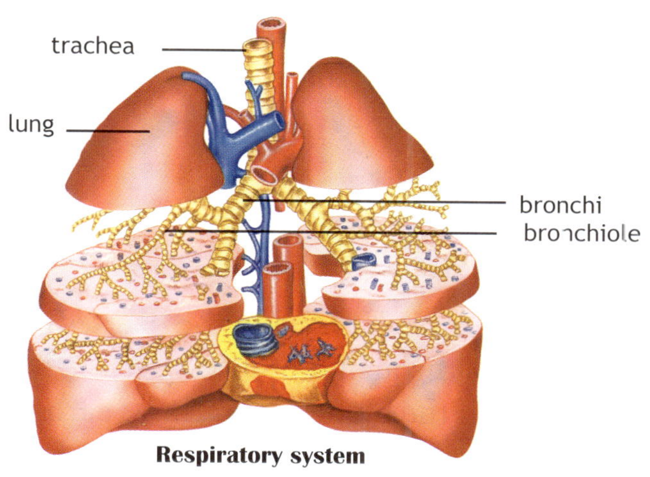

Respiratory system

Tiny air sacs at the end of each bronchiole is called ______.

Heart

The heart is a muscular organ located in the middle of the chest. It is an organ of the circulatory system. It collects deoxygenated blood and pumps oxygenated blood into the body through various arteries and veins. The arteries and veins are called blood vessels.

Blood

Blood contains blood cells and plasma. Red blood cells, white blood cells, and platelets are types of blood cells. Plasma is a fluid in which blood cells float and travel. Red blood cells carry oxygen to the body. White blood cells defend the body from germs. Platelets help in the process of blood clotting.

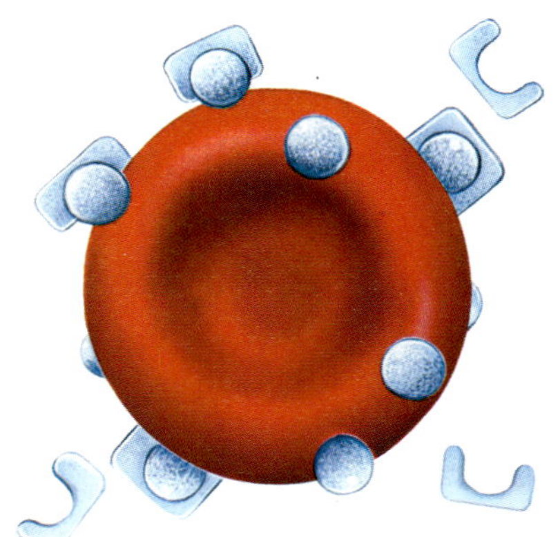

Blood Circulation

The lungs send oxygen-rich blood to the heart. This blood is then sent to all body parts through blood vessels. The body utilises all the oxygen present in the blood and releases carbon dioxide into it. The heart then sends this deoxygenated blood to the lungs for its purification.

Heart

The heart has four chambers. The upper chambers are called atria, and the lower chambers are called ventricles. The atria receive blood from the body and lungs, while the ventricles squeeze blood out to the body and lungs.

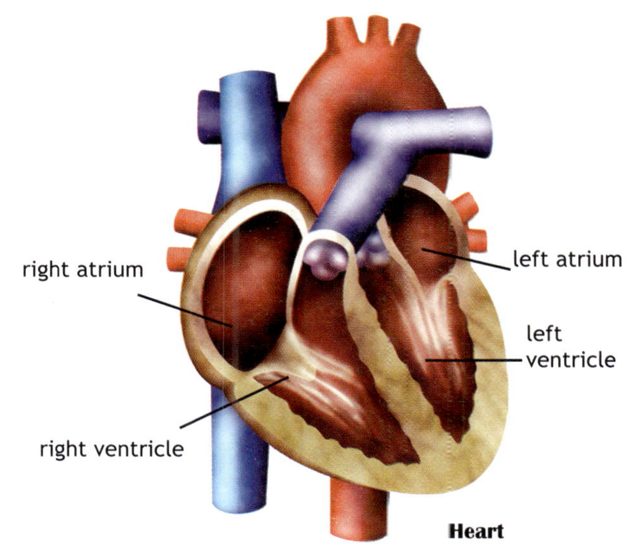

Heart

Arteries and Veins

Arteries carry oxygenated blood from the heart to all parts of body and veins carry deoxygenated blood from body parts to the heart.

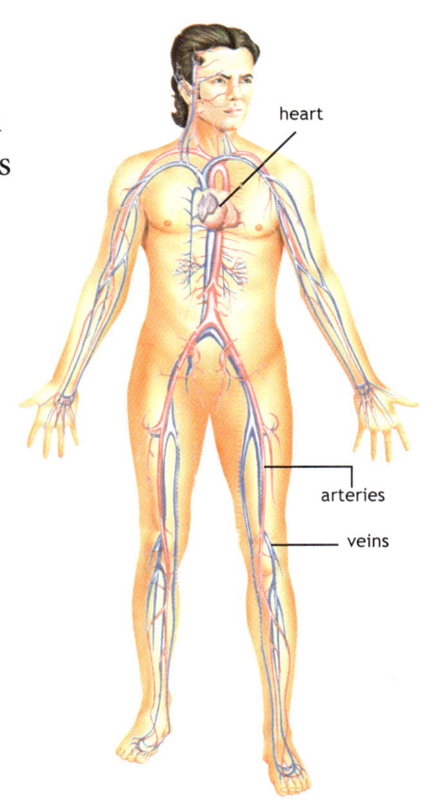

- It takes less than 60 seconds to pump blood to all parts of the body.
- While resting, a person's heart beats 60 to 80 times in a minute.
- Our heart beats around 100,000 times a day.

How many chambers does the heart have?

Think and React

The nervous system, which enables thinking and reacting to various situations, consists of the brain, spinal cord, and nerves. The brain serves as the control centre, while the nerves, running throughout the body, carry messages, and the spinal cord creates a link between the brain and the nerves.

Neurons

Nerves are made up of millions of nerve cells called neurons. They are connected to each other through branches coming out of them. Some neurons pass information from the sense organs to the brain, while others send messages from the brain to other parts of the body.

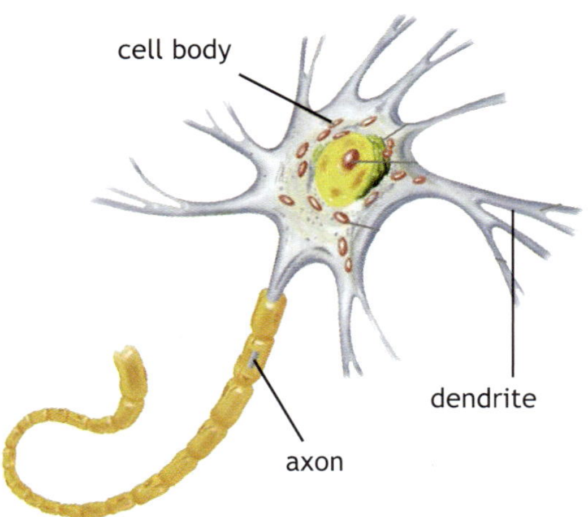

Structure of a neuron

Facts

- The right half of the cerebrum controls the left side of the body; the left half controls the right side.
- There are about 30,000 million neurons in the human body.
- The brain is made up of 100 billion (plus) nerve cells and other cells.

The Network of Nerves

Nerves connect the brain to the rest of the body by forming a network inside the body. Cranial nerves come out of the brain and control the movement of muscles. Spinal nerves branch out of the spinal cord to different parts of the body.

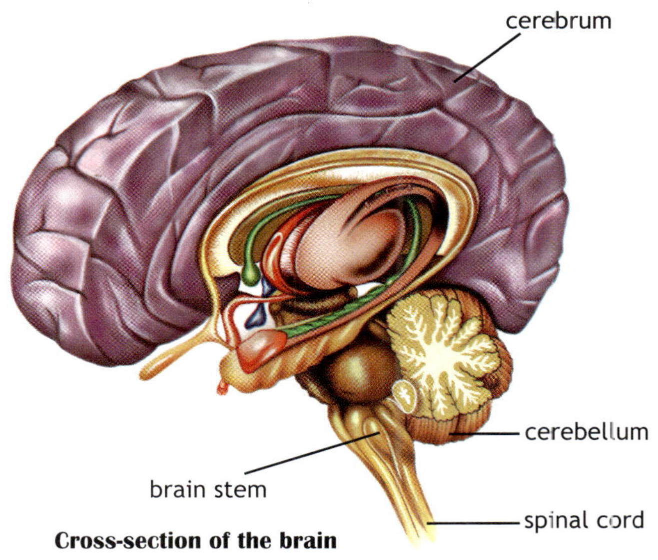

Cross-section of the brain

Brain

The cerebrum, cerebellum, and brain stem are the three major parts of the brain. The cerebrum is the largest part and controls memory, thinking, and reasoning. The cerebellum controls the balance and movement of the body. The brain stem connects the brain to the spinal cord and controls major body functions.

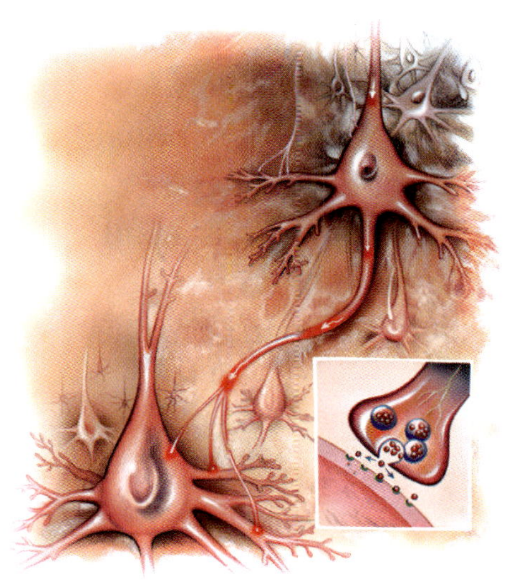

 **Name the largest part of the brain.**

Clearing Waste

The human body produces a lot of waste while performing different functions. This waste is removed by the urinary system. The kidneys, bladder, and ureters are the major organs of the urinary system.

Kidneys Make Urine

When the heart pumps out blood to the body, about 20 percent of it goes to the kidneys. Kidneys have more than one million tiny filters known as nephrons, which are the functional units of the kidneys. Each nephron has a ball of small blood vessels called Bowman's capsule, and small tubes. Here, the blood is purified as waste products are removed from the blood to form urine.

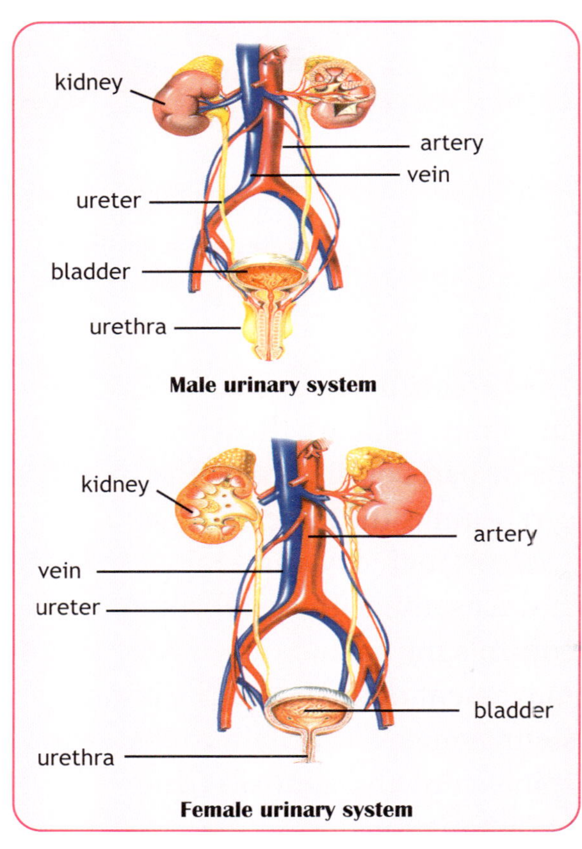

Male urinary system

Female urinary system

Bladder

Urine goes to the bladder from the kidneys through a long tube. The bladder is where urine is stored. It expands when it is full. The walls of the bladder contract to let the urine pass out of the body.

Urea

Urea is the chief component of urine. It is a waste product released from the breakdown of proteins. Foods such as meat, chicken and pulses are rich in protein.

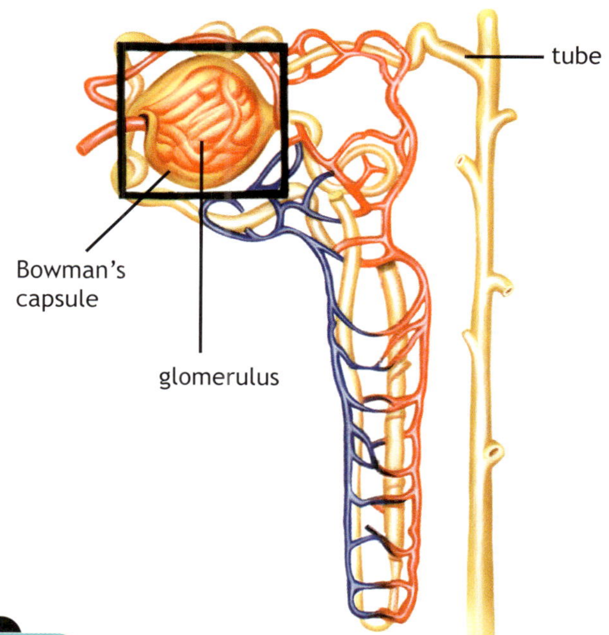

Structure of nephron

- The kidneys are about the size of a computer mouse.
- The kidneys filter about 3.7 liters to 5.6 liters (1 to 1.5 gallons) of blood 20-25 times in a day.
- The bladder can hold about two cups of urine easily for 2 to 5 hours.

How many nephrons are there in a kidney?

Bony Framework

Our body is built on a bony framework called the skeleton. The skeleton provides support and structure for the body. All the organs inside the body are protected by the skeleton.

Inside Bones

Bones have a thin outer membrane that covers and nourishes them. The smooth layer inside it is made of a hard material called compact bone. The next layer is the spongy bone, which is stronger and lighter. The innermost structure of a bone is the bone marrow. It makes millions of new blood cells continuously.

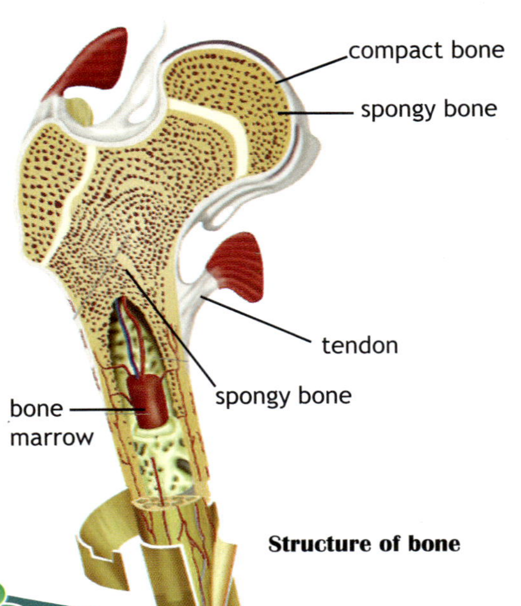

Structure of bone

Facts

- The femur or the thigh bone is the largest bone in our body.
- Bones become strongest by the age of 20.
- A baby is born with about 300 bones, which, as they grow up, fuse together, leaving an adult with 206 bones.

Supporting Spine

The spine, also known as the backbone of our body, allows us to bend, twist, and stand upright. Comprising 33 bones, it encases and protects the spinal cord.

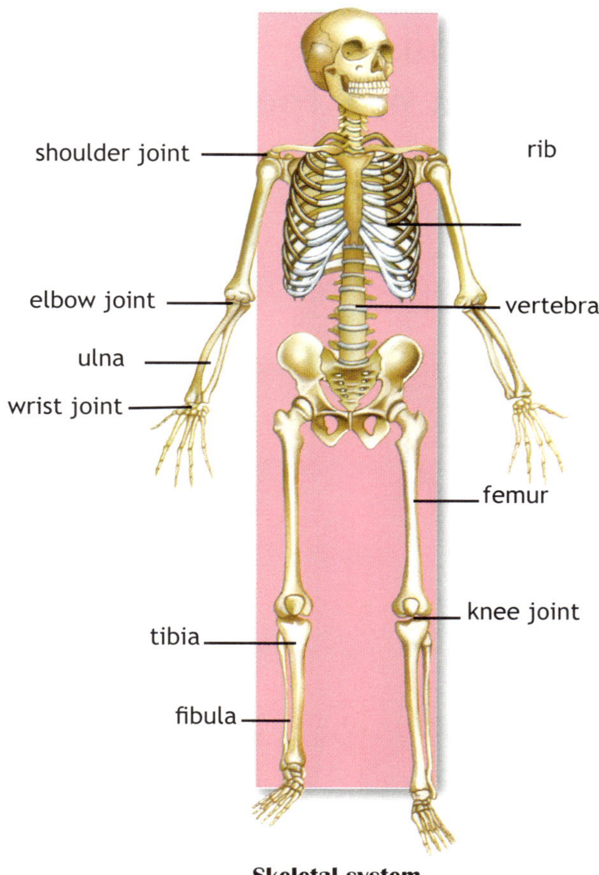

Skeletal system

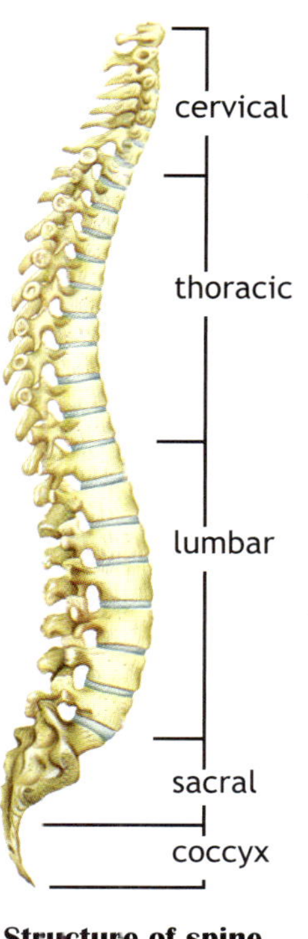

Structure of spine

Joints

The place where two bones meet is called a joint. Joints have a special fluid between them. This fluid helps the joints move freely. Some joints are movable, while others are not. Ligaments are fibrous tissues that connect two bones.

New blood cells are made inside ________.

Muscles and Movement

Muscles help us do all our daily life activities. They contract and relax to produce body movements. There are three types of muscles: smooth muscles, heart muscles, and skeletal muscles. Smooth muscles are found in major organs like the stomach.

Skeletal Muscles

Skeletal muscles, which are attached to bones, facilitate body movement and provide strength. The smallest muscles are located in the ear, while one of the longest muscles in the body is the sartorius muscle in the thigh.

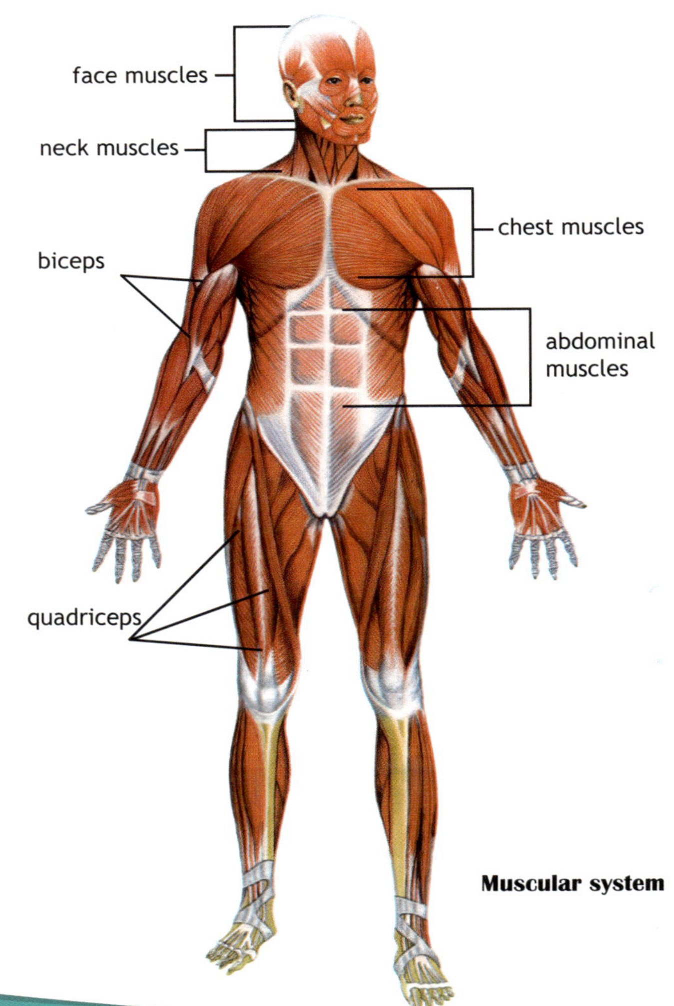

Muscular system

Major Muscle Movements

Small muscles in the face contract to create a variety of facial expressions. The neck muscles allow movements up, down, left, and right. Arm muscles enable us to pull and lift objects, while thigh and leg muscles are essential for running, jumping, and walking.

Joining Muscles

Tendons are tough tissue cords that connect muscles to bones. When a muscle contracts, the tendon pulls the attached bone, resulting in movement.

- We have more than 100 muscles in our face.
- It takes 34 muscles to frown and 13 muscles to smile.
- We need 72 muscles to speak.

Tendon

How many types of muscles are there in human body?

Birth and Growth

A baby takes nine months to be born. After birth, a baby gradually passes through various developmental stages before reaching adulthood, experiencing many changes during these years of growth.

Life Begins

Life begins when a sperm from a man fertilises an egg from a woman. Sperms are produced in the testes, while eggs are produced in the ovaries, which are the reproductive organs in males and females, respectively. The fertilised egg then divides, forming a ball of cells known as an embryo.

- The size of our eyes remains the same throughout our life.
- Our nose and ears grow throughout life.
- The heart of a developing baby starts beating after 18 days.

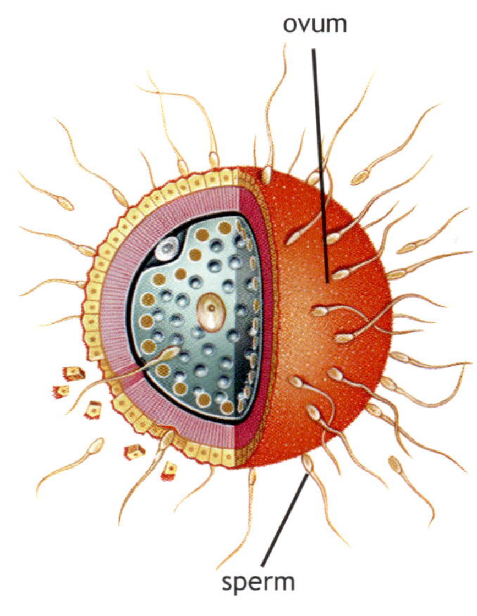

Beginning of life

Mother and Baby

The fetus is attached to the mother by the placenta, located on the wall of the uterus, and is connected to the fetus via the umbilical cord. The mother supplies essential nutrients and oxygen to the baby through this cord. When a baby is born, the cord is cut, leaving the navel on the baby's abdomen.

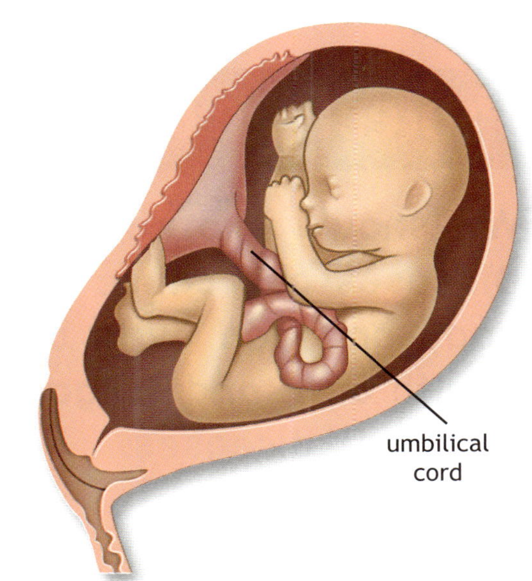

The Developing Baby

Inside the uterus, the embryo grows into a baby. Over time, different body parts, such as the heart, brain, lungs, hands, and legs, begin to develop. At this stage, the baby is approximately 2.5 centimetres (about 1 inch) in length. After the completion of 38 weeks, the baby is typically ready to be born.

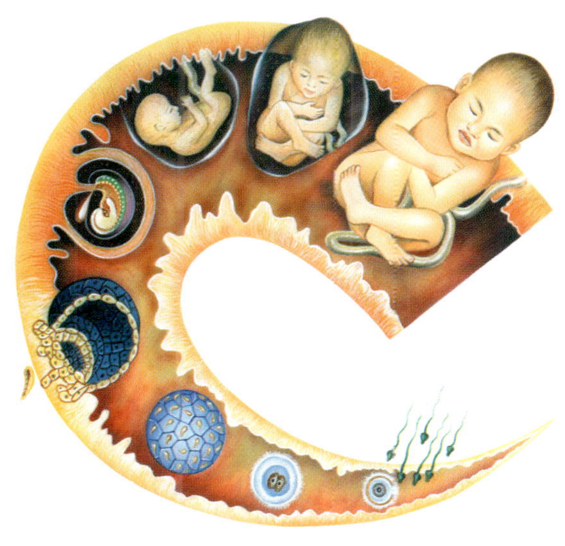

Development of a baby

 **Ears and nose never stops growing. (True or False)**

Protect the Body

We should protect our body from diseases. Diseases can cause harm to any part of our body and can even cause death. Medicines, health care and surgery are the ways to fight and cure diseases.

Vaccination

Vaccinating children can prevent certain diseases, such as chickenpox, smallpox, and polio. Vaccinations work by injecting tiny amounts of dead or weakened germs, allowing white blood cells to recognise and create a defence against these germs.

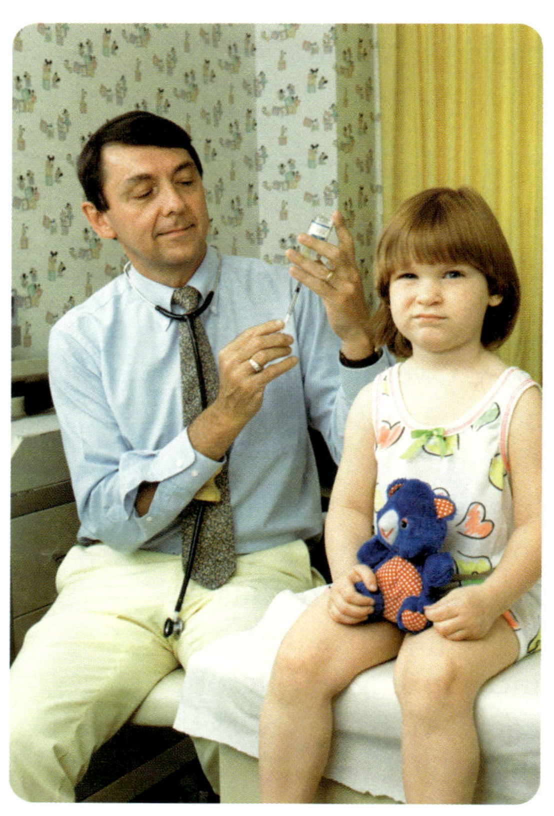

Eat Healthy

A person should eat lots of fruits and vegetables as they are rich sources of vitamins and minerals. Eating healthy food makes the body stronger and more resistant to diseases. A healthy body can fight off disease-causing germs. For a fit and healthy body, a person should avoid overeating junk food.

Simple Ways to Prevent Diseases

- Always wash your hands before and after eating.
- Drink clean and filtered water.
- Use tissues or handkerchiefs when sneezing or coughing.
- Get regular vaccinations.

- In 95 percent cases of polio, no symptoms occur.
- A cancer patient may have elevated white blood cell counts, with as many as 50,000 cells in a single drop of blood, compared to the normal range of 7,000 to 25,000 cells per drop.

Can polio be prevented by vaccination?

Keeping Healthy

Nutritious food and regular exercise are vital for maintaining health throughout our lives. A daily diet should include all essential nutrients for proper growth, and regular exercise helps the heart supply oxygen efficiently to the body.

Balanced Diet

A balanced diet contains all nutrients in the correct amounts. It keeps us healthy and allows us to live a longer life. Carbohydrates, proteins, fats, vitamins, and minerals are the major nutrients that form a balanced diet.

Fitness Exercises

Exercise keeps our body fit. The heart beats faster and the lungs expand harder during exercise, which makes them stronger. Running, cycling, jumping, walking, and swimming are common exercises. Walking keeps us fit and swimming makes our muscles stronger.

Key Points to Remain Healthy

- Eat a lot of fruits and vegetables. Eat fruit with breakfast and as snacks, and eat vegetables as salads with lunch and dinner.
- Drink plenty of water.
- Drink milk to grow strong bones.
- Limit your time watching television and playing video games.
- Play your favourite sport or activity regularly.

- Regular exercise reduces the risk of heart disease, diabetes, and cancer.
- Fruits and vegetables contain vitamins and fibre.

A diet rich in all vitamins and minerals is called a ____________.

Glands that Help

Endocrine system helps to keep the body working steadily and properly. It is made up of different glands that produce chemicals called hormones which perform different jobs in the body. Hormones are a type of messenger that carries messages throughout the body. Endocrine system affects every cell and plays a vital role in the functions of the body.

Endocrine Glands

Like other organ systems, endocrine system is made of many parts called endocrine glands. The main endocrine glands are listed below.

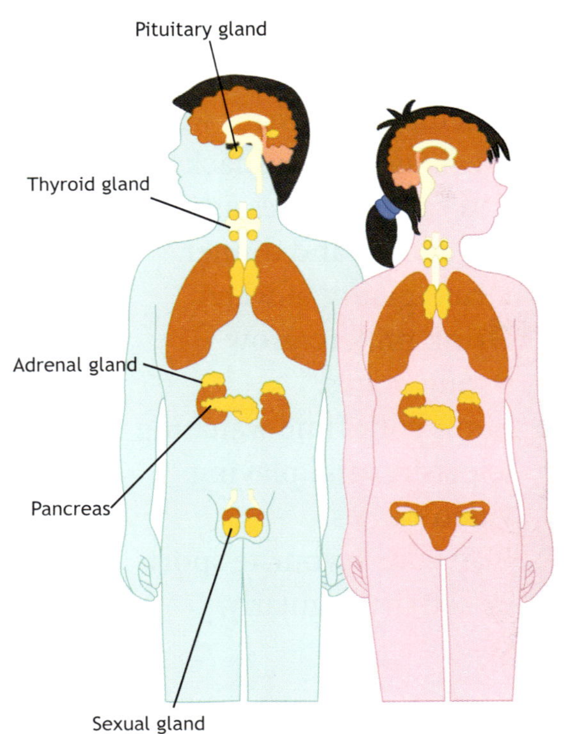

Pineal gland

It produces the hormone melatonin, which regulates sleep.

Pituitary gland

It is about the size of a pea and is located beneath the hypothalamus. It regulates and controls the working of other endocrine glands.

Thyroid and parathyroid

They are located below the larynx, or voice box, in the neck. They release hormones which look after the body's metabolism and level of calcium.

- The doctors who treat diseases and infections related to the endocrine system are called endocrinologists.
- On the whole, the endocrine glands release more than 20 main hormones essential for the body.

Adrenal glands

They lie above the kidneys. These glands produce hormones that control the salt and water balance in the body.

Reproductive glands

They produce different types of reproductive hormones in girls and boys.

Where is pituitary gland located?

Body's Defence System

Immune system is the body's defense system. It protects the body from infection and disease causing germs. The immune system along with various body parts helps in trapping and killing harmful germs. Some of the body parts such as skin, eyes, stomach have their own ways to defend the body.

Skin

The skin is the body's outermost layer, coming into contact with millions of germs and providing a primary defence barrier. Unless there is a cut or bruise, the germs won't enter the body.

Eyes

The eyelashes and tears in the eyes also serve as defences against germs, with tears containing chemicals that can kill harmful microorganisms.

Nose and Throat

Just like the skin, mucus is present inside the nose and throat, acting as a barrier to germs. Mucous traps dirt and dust, and prevents germs from entering the body.

Blood

Blood is made up of red blood cells and white blood cells. White blood cells (WBC) fight off germs and infections. Hence, they are also known as the warriors of the body.

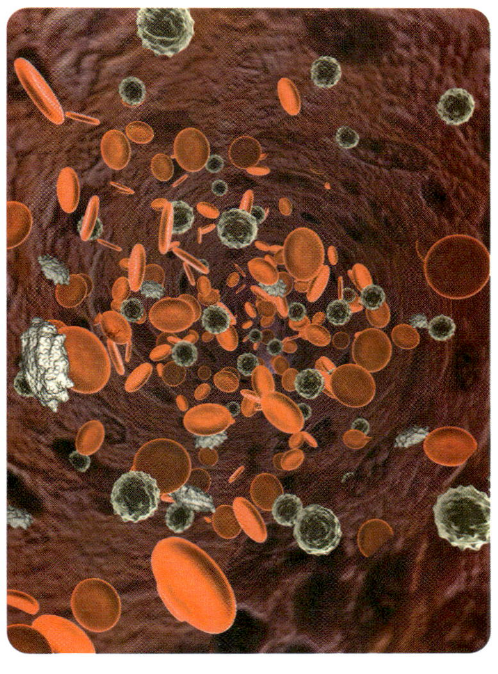

Facts

- The study of immune system and its functions is called immunology.
- Pus is a mixture of dead white blood cells and germs.
- Pus is typically white due to the presence of white blood cells and can turn yellow due to dead cells, germs, and immune proteins.

? _________ **blood cells are called warriors of the body.**

Falling Sick

Diseases can be caused by germs. They can also be genetic or related to nutritional deficiencies. Germs like bacteria and virus cause infectious diseases. Infectious diseases are easily transmitted from one person to another. Diseases that arise due to genetic problems or nutritional deficiencies are non-infectious. They cannot be transferred from one person to another.

Infectious Diseases

Infectious diseases, also known as contagious diseases, are caused by germs and can be transmitted from one person to another through actions like hugging, touching, or consuming something infected. Common items such as towels and pillows can also facilitate the spread of these diseases, with the common cold and flu being typical examples.

Non-infectious Diseases

Non-infectious diseases can be caused by factors such as environment, lifestyle, or genetic inheritance. For example, heart diseases may result from a poor diet, a lack of exercise, a family history of the disease, or a sedentary lifestyle. Diabetes and cancer are other examples of non-infectious diseases.

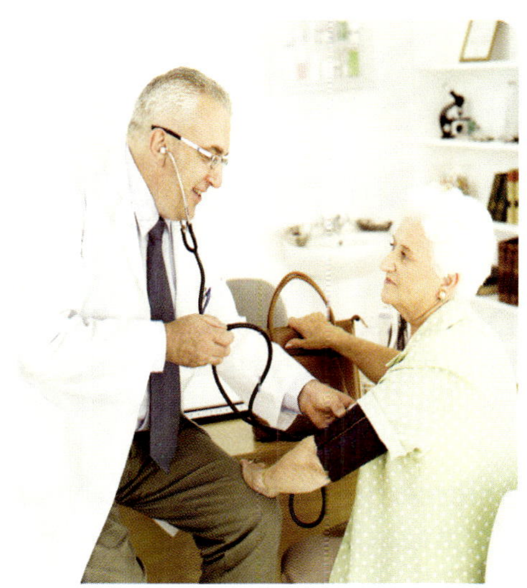

Deficiency Diseases

Deficiency diseases, a category of non-infectious diseases, are caused by a lack of vitamins and minerals in the diet. Common examples include anemia, which is caused by iron deficiency, and night blindness, resulting from a vitamin A deficiency.

- Sunlight is the natural source of vitamin D.
- The body creates vitamin D when it is exposed to sunlight.
- Flu is the common name for influenza.
- Heart diseases are also called cardiovascular diseases.

Common cold is not a contagious disease. (True or False)

Glossary

Metabolism: a biological process where the body converts food into energy

Diabetes: a chronic condition characterised by elevated blood sugar levels, often due to issues with insulin production or response

Microorganism: extremely small living organisms, invisible to the naked eye, and observable only under a microscope

Environment: the surroundings or conditions in which a person, animal, or plant lives or operates, including elements like air, water, and soil

Blood clotting: a process where blood turns from a liquid to a gel, forming a clot, which helps stop bleeding

Blood vessel: any of the tubular structures carrying blood throughout the body, including arteries, veins, and capillaries

Capillary: tiny blood vessels connecting arterioles and venules, enabling exchange of gases, nutrients, and waste between blood and tissues

Chamber: a compartment or enclosed space, often referring to areas within organs or structures

Cord: thick string or rope

Eardrum: a thin, tightly stretched membrane in the ear that vibrates in response to sound waves

Cuticle: the layer of skin at the base of fingernails and toenails

Follicle: a small cavity in the skin, especially in the dermis, from which a hair develops

Framework: a structure that holds something

Genetic: related to genes which are chemicals present in the cells of the body

Gland: pertaining to genes, which are units of heredity in living organisms located in the DNA.

Dentical: similar in appearance

Navel: a small round place in the middle of the stomach

Network: a complex, interconnected group of systems.

Purify: to remove contaminants or impurities

Sac: bag-like or pouch-like

Saliva: a watery secretion in the mouth that lubricates and breaks down food, aiding in digestion

Spinal cord: a long, thin, tubular bundle of nerves and supporting cells that extends from the brain down the back, part of the central nervous system

Stomach juice: a type of liquid produced by the stomach which helps in digestion of food

Surgery: treatment of a disease or an injury through an operation

Vibration: a quick back and forth movement

Answers

Page No. 51	Centre
Page No. 53	Skin
Page No. 55	Retina
Page No. 57	Epidermis
Page No. 59	True
Page No. 61	Food pipe
Page No. 63	Alveoli
Page No. 65	Four
Page No. 67	Cerebrum
Page No. 69	More than a million
Page No. 71	Bone marrow
Page No. 73	Three
Page No. 75	True
Page No. 77	Yes
Page No. 79	Balanced diet
Page No. 81	Beneath the hypothalamus
Page No. 83	White
Page No. 85	False